RYAN'S CROSSING

Ryan's Crossing

by
Carrie Daws

Ambassador International
GREENVILLE, SOUTH CAROLINA & BELFAST, NORTHERN IRELAND

www.ambassador-international.com

RYAN'S CROSSING

Printed in the United States of America

ISBN: 978-1-62020-102-2
eISBN: 978-1-62020-152-7

Unless otherwise indicated, all Scripture was taken from the HOLY BIBLE, NEW INTERNATIONAL VERSION. Copyright 1973, 1978, 1984 by International Bible Society. Used by permission of Zondervan. All rights reserved.

Cover Design and Page Layout by Matthew Mulder

AMBASSADOR INTERNATIONAL
Emerald House
427 Wade Hampton Blvd.
Greenville, SC 29609, USA
www.ambassador-international.com

AMBASSADOR BOOKS
The Mount
2 Woodstock Link
Belfast, BT6 8DD, Northern Ireland, UK
www.ambassador-international.com

The colophon is a trademark of Ambassador

My son, if you accept my words and store up my commands within you,
turning your ear to wisdom and applying your heart to understanding,
and if you call out for insight and cry aloud for understanding, and if
you look for it as for silver and search for it as for hidden treasure, then
you will understand the fear of the Lord and find the knowledge of God.

For the Lord gives wisdom, and from His mouth come
knowledge and understanding.

Proverbs 2:1–6

Chapter I

THE BLACK MUSTANG ROARED INTO town, its small block 302 engine disturbing the peaceful January afternoon in Crossing, Oregon. Ryan Griffin looked out the windshield, taking in the picket fences. *Just another small Oregon town,* he thought.

Slowing as he entered the square, he looked for Micah's Hardware where he was supposed to meet his parents. As he parked in front of the blue, two-story building, he turned off the engine and sat quiet for a minute. *Rachel,* he thought. *After ten years, they actually found my sister.*

He opened his door and stepped out as a sheriff's truck pulled up behind him. A uniformed man got out, looking him and the Fastback over.

"Nice ride," the sheriff said.

"Thanks," said Ryan, taking in the neat uniform that wasn't starched and pressed to crisp seams. *Professional, but still casual.*

"What year?"

"Sixty-eight."

"Working on restoring it?"

"Yeah."

"Didn't sound completely stock as you drove down McKillican Street back there." The sheriff turned from inspecting the car to look directly at Ryan, his breath clearly visible in the chilly air.

"No, sir. I've upgraded it a bit here and there."

The sheriff dipped his head a little. "As long as the upgrades keep within the legal speed limits, you'll have no problem with me."

Ryan nodded his dark head at the sheriff. "Yes, sir."

The sheriff walked back around to his truck door and took one more look at Ryan's car. "Really like that red pin striping down the side. Nice choice."

"Thanks."

Ryan watched the sheriff drive away before turning to Micah's. He squared his shoulders and mentally prepared himself to greet his dad. *It's only for a week,* he thought.

Just as he took his first steps toward the store, his younger brother Keith burst through the doors.

"Ryan!"

Ryan smiled. "Hey!"

Keith slammed into him, embracing him in a hug. *He's done some growing since I last saw him.* Keith now stood almost even with Ryan's five foot, nine inch height, although the skinniness of youth still encompassed his rib cage.

"Can we not wait six months between visits?" said Keith. "I missed you at Christmas!"

"I know," said Ryan. "It was really busy at work. I ended up working most of December."

"Come on, Mom's excited to see you!"

Keith led Ryan up the three steps and through the front door. Aisles of tools angled to lead people to the front counter lined the old wood floor. An older man was unpacking saw blades near the cash register.

"Hey, Mr. Micah! This is my brother, Ryan."

Micah looked up from the box. "So I see."

"Mom!" said Keith. "Mom, he's here!"

"You yell a bit louder there, boy, and I suspect Hood Village'll hear ya right good," said Micah.

Ryan stopped to look at the gruff man, his paramedic brain assessing Micah before considering the man's demeanor. *Tall, maybe 6 feet. Probably just barely 140 pounds. Older, maybe 65. Reminds me a lot of Clint Eastwood.*

"Ryan!" said his mom as she came from the back of the store. She gave him a hug, going up on her tiptoes so her chin fit comfortably over his shoulder.

"Hey, Mom. You look good." *She's put on a little weight! She's not all skin and bones any more.*

"Thanks."

Her smile took in her whole face, which had a bit more color than he remembered, and her short brown hair bounced. *Finding Rachel has been good for her.*

"I can't wait for you to see Amber!" said Keith. "She's really cool. And she remembers that old tire swing we found!"

"Amber?" said Ryan.

"Yes, your sister goes by Amber now," his mother explained. "I think bad memories made her switch to her middle name, but Peter is changing all that."

"Her fiancé, right?" said Ryan.

"Wait 'til you meet him!" said Keith. "He's really great with wood. He's going to teach me some. He knows all about the trees and stuff. Can tell you just about anything you want to know about the forest."

"You always this spastic around your brother, boy?" said Micah.

"Sorry," said Keith. "It's just there's so much to tell him!"

"No sense overwhelmin' him all at once. You'll scare him out of town just so's he can get a moment's peace! Now get on wit' ya. You still got work to do."

Ryan raised his eyebrows at Micah's treatment of Keith. His mother laid a hand on his arm.

"Don't mind him," she said softly. "He's all grizzly bear on the outside, but in truth, your brother has brought some life back into him. He just lost his wife last summer, and Allie says he was really struggling. They were married over forty years."

Ryan just nodded his head like he understood. "Allie?"

"His daughter-in-law," said Victoria. "She works just on the other side of the square and stops over almost everyday to check on him."

"Dedicated girl," said Ryan. *Or controlling,* he thought.

"Come on," said Victoria. "Let's leave these men to their work. Would you like to wait for your dad or go meet Amber? I believe she's still in town."

"Where is Dad?" said Ryan.

"He's over at the newspaper sending off a couple stories. We're staying upstairs for now, and Micah doesn't have Internet access here."

His dad's ability to write from anywhere made chasing his daughter these last several years possible. As long as he made his deadlines with quality stories, editors from the various publications were happy to send the check to whatever location he dictated.

"If Dad's working, then don't bother him."

"All right. Then let's go meet your sister. I think she said she'd be working with Allie all afternoon." Victoria walked to the back and grabbed her coat off a peg, swinging it around her shoulders. "We're going to see Amber, Micah."

"Don't you go fallin' on no ice patches," said Micah as he cut through the tape on the bottom of the box and laid it flat.

"I'll be careful," said Victoria with a tolerant smile.

Ryan held the door open for her then offered his arm as they walked down the block.

"She's just down here at the law office," said Victoria.

Ryan was shocked. "She's a lawyer?"

"No. You see, the town lawyer is Andy, Micah's son. And his wife, Allie, is the town accountant. Amber is thinking about going back to school, but in the meantime is taking some lessons from Allie so she can help out more at the logging office."

Ryan shook his head. "Town lawyer, son of town hardware store owner, married to town accountant teaching my sister how to take over at the town logging office? You really know a lot about these people."

Victoria laughed. "I suppose it does sound that way. Crossing is a small town, and most of these people have lived here their whole lives. Once you are accepted by one of them, the rest just kind of adopt you."

"You've been adopted?"

"Yes, I suppose we have. Oh, Ryan, this town. These people." She moved in closer to Ryan as a breeze swirled around them. "They are just incredible. Like a family. I cannot tell you what a blessing it is to live here among them in the Cascade Mountains."

Ryan didn't quite catch his Mom's enthusiasm. "Live here? So you're moving here now?" He looked around, raising his eyebrows at the old architecture in the town square. *They all seemed to be well maintained, but the newest building has to be circa 1950s.*

"Yes. We're still working out all the details, but Micah's letting us live above the store until we figure it all out. It's not much right now because Micah's been using the upstairs for storage for many years. But we're getting it cleaned out."

Ryan wasn't sure what to say. *They are moving again. Maybe if Rachel's here, it will be permanent this time. Wonder how long until Dad expects me to move here too?*

"Micah actually owns an old log cabin just outside of town that we may purchase from him. It needs some work—they stopped using it a couple years before his wife died. The walls are solid. It's not that big, but Keith is getting older. We won't need much after he moves out."

"Sounds like you've already decided."

"Perhaps." Victoria stopped outside a two-story frame building with a picture window in front. "Well, here we are," said Victoria, looking up with anticipation in her face. "Are you ready?"

"I guess." *Here goes nothing.*

Chapter 2

RYAN HELD THE DOOR OPEN for his mom and then stepped in behind her. The small office included a receptionist's desk with a woman sitting behind it studying something on her computer screen. The room was also furnished with four chairs that lined the walls, and a small table with a coffee pot and a few mugs. Stairs tucked away in one corner of the office led to the second floor, and two open doors were before him, one to Ryan's left beside the receptionist's desk and the other slightly to his right. As the door closed behind him, a brown and white Australian shepherd came to stand in the doorway to his right.

"Hello, Rose," said Victoria to the woman at the desk. "How are you this Thursday afternoon?"

Ryan watched the hair on the dog's brown back raise slightly.

"Doing good. I'm just taking care of a few of the year-end things. Must get some of these older things filed away so I can make room for this year."

"Of course. Is Amber here? I thought I saw the Yagers drop her off earlier."

A young woman came up behind the dog. "Mom?"

Short and skinny, five feet, two inches. 110-115 pounds. Mid-twenties... Rachel? Ryan paused in his assessment to look at the woman his sister had become. Her long, dark hair fashionably layered to frame her face, rich chocolate eyes full of life. Wow.

"Ryan?" said Amber. Her eyes seemed to be watering slightly, but she hung back with the dog.

"Guilty," said Ryan. *Now what? Is she waiting on me to make the first move?*

"Sass," said Amber, looking down at the dog beside her and laying her hand on top of the dog's head. "Friend, girl." The dog immediately sat, although Ryan noticed it didn't take its eyes off of him.

Amber crossed to where they were standing. She seemed unsure of herself, and Ryan wasn't sure what to do, either.

"It's good to see you," said Amber.

"Yeah," said Ryan. "You too."

A trim, curly-haired blonde just a couple inches taller than Amber appeared in the doorway near the dog.

"Hello, Allie," said Victoria. "Our son Ryan is finally here!"

"Hi, Mrs. Griffin." Allie walked forward to join the group near the reception desk. She held her hand out to Ryan. "It's nice to meet you."

Ryan returned the firm handshake. "Thanks."

Amber looked up at Ryan. "You grew tall!"

"You didn't," said Ryan.

"Thanks." She smiled at him, shaking her head just a bit. "When'd you get into town?"

"About thirty minutes ago."

"Still getting your bearings, huh?" Amber looked at her mom. "Do you guys have any plans for dinner yet?"

"No," said Victoria. "Your dad is filing a couple stories, so he doesn't even know Ryan's here yet."

"Okay. Well, you know, Mom, that Faye will want all of you over for dinner. She can't wait to meet Ryan."

"Who's Faye?" said Ryan.

"Peter's mother," said Victoria.

Amber smiled at her brother. "She loves a party. And frequently uses any excuse she can think of to cook for an army and have people over to eat it. If you guys don't come over tonight, then she'll insist on this weekend."

"I don't think we have any plans tonight," said Victoria, "but I really should check with your dad. Are you too tired from traveling, Ryan?"

"Mom, I can do whatever. McWilliam's not that far of a drive, and I haven't worked since Tuesday. I just need to find a place to stay."

"That won't be hard," said Amber. "Crossing doesn't really have any hotels, but Faye has an extra room if you don't mind staying down the hall from me. Or Peter has space if you'd rather live bachelor-style with him."

"We are planning to clean out space this weekend for you to stay with us," said Victoria. "If you can manage with Amber or Peter for a couple days, you can always stay with us after that."

"Whatever you're comfortable with," said Amber.

"Amber," said Allie, "why don't we call it a day so you can enjoy your family? We can get together again next week if you have any time."

"Sounds good, Allie. Thanks! Let me grab my coat, Mom, and we'll go find Dad."

The trio left the law office with the dog, Sassy, close behind and headed further around the square to the newspaper storefront.

"How long have you had the dog?" said Ryan.

Amber giggled. "She adopted me shortly after I got here in November."

"That's twice now I've heard that," said Ryan.

"What?" said Amber.

"Adopted," said Ryan.

"Well, she didn't give me much choice," said Amber. "She's really Peter's dog."

"Did you start giving her treats or something?" said Ryan.

"I didn't do anything," said Amber. "In fact, when I first got here, I was afraid of her. But it seemed the more I avoided her, the more she wanted to hang around me. Now she follows me pretty much everywhere."

"It appears that you've gotten over your fear," said Ryan.

"At least where Sassy's concerned, I guess," said Amber.

"If you two wait here," said Victoria, "I'll run inside and ask Owen if your dad is still here."

Without waiting for an answer, she disappeared through the doorway, leaving Ryan and Amber standing on the front walk mostly cleared of snow.

"So what do you do?" said Amber.

"Besides pick on annoying brunettes?"

"I was hoping you'd outgrown that."

Ryan grinned at her. "I'm a paramedic."

"Really! Did that require a lot of school?"

"Depends, I guess. Nothing like a doctor, but it's still hundreds of hours of training, ambulance calls, and clinicals."

"I'm impressed," said Amber, pushing her mitten-clad hands into her coat pockets.

"Thanks. How about you?"

"Not much. I never finished high school, which is pretty limiting on the job market. But, I'm thinking about taking some online accounting classes through Oregon State so I can help out more at the logging office. I have to get my GED first, but Allie says I'm picking up on what she's teaching me pretty quickly."

"Does that mean you're going to stay here?"

"Yeah. Peter plans to take over his dad's business. I don't see us moving anywhere."

"Ryan!" Thomas Griffin came out of the newspaper office, backpack slung over his shoulder, and hugged his son. His short-cropped grey hair was a bit disheveled, an indication that his editor had requested some quick revisions.

"Hey, Dad," said Ryan. "Get your stories filed?"

"Yes. Now my evening is free to spend with my three children!" He placed one hand on Ryan's shoulder and wrapped his other arm around Amber's waist.

"That sounds so nice," said Victoria.

"Yes, it does," said Thomas.

"You want to come out to dinner at Faye's, Dad?" said Amber.

"I would not turn down her cooking," said Thomas.

"Are you sure she won't mind, Amber?" said Victoria.

"Positive. I'll call her when we get to Micah's if it makes you feel better."

"Well then," said Thomas, "what are we waiting for?"

The group turned to make their way around the square.

"So how was the weather in McWilliam?" Thomas asked.

"About normal." Ryan shrugged. "We got a couple inches throughout December, but most of that was closer to Christmas."

"So you had a lot of accidents?"

Ryan's internal radar sensed this was leading to his not showing up for the holidays. *Keep your words in check,* he reminded himself. "Always do, Dad, but not always because of the snow. People also tend to do more social and emotional drinking around Christmas and New Year's."

As they approached Micah's, a dark grey Jeep Grand Cherokee parked in front of the store. Ryan watched a man just a couple inches taller than himself get out. *He's 165-170 pounds, late twenties. Muscular, maybe athletic.*

"Peter!" said Amber.

Ryan watched as his sister ran over and waited for him at the edge of the snow berm.

"Hey, my beautiful Ray," said Peter. He took both Amber's hands in his, kissing the top of one mitten-covered hand.

"Come meet Ryan," said Amber.

Peter wrapped his left arm around Amber's shoulder and turned to greet the others.

So this is the man who finally trapped my sister in one place.

"Ryan, this is Peter."

Peter extended his hand to Ryan. "Nice to finally meet you."

"Thanks," said Ryan.

"Did you drive up in that?" said Peter, motioning to the Mustang.

"Yeah."

Peter left Amber's side to look more closely at the car, whistling in appreciation. "She's incredible."

"Thanks. It's a bit of a hobby."

"Do you prefer doing body work, or more the mechanics of it?" said Peter.

"Definitely mechanics. I looked around for a while until I found one with a decent body so I wouldn't have to do too much to it."

"Does she give you much trouble in the snow?"

"She doesn't really like the fresh stuff, but packed down isn't too bad. I keep good 245s on the back wheels and replace them with studless winter tires when the snow hits."

Peter looked in the driver's window. "Stick shift! Nice!"

"Yeah, I bought it as an automatic but changed it out to a five-speed."

"Really nice," said Peter. "I've always liked the running pony's interior."

Amber stepped up to Peter's side and touched his arm. "I was going to call your mom to see if she minded guests for dinner."

"Actually, that's part of my errand to come get you. When I left the office, Mom asked me to swing by here and see if everyone wanted to come out tonight. It's Mexican night, and she said she'd made far too much of the chicken mixture to make only one pan of enchiladas."

"Wonderful," said Thomas.

Ryan laughed at his dad. "She must be a good cook."

"The best," said Thomas. "Next to your mother, of course."

"She really is very good," said Amber.

"Are you sure it's not too much?" said Victoria.

"You have to stop worrying so much, Vic," said Thomas.

"Mom wouldn't ask if she didn't mean it," said Peter. "And she said to tell you that she already has dessert waiting to go in the oven."

"What more do we need to know?" said Thomas, looking at the others.

Victoria laughed. "All right. Let me get Keith before your stomach leaves us all standing here!"

Chapter 3

RYAN TOOK UP THE REAR position of the caravan as they followed Peter to his parents' home. His mind was reeling with the bits of information he'd already gleaned from the short time he'd had with his family.

The family looks great! I don't remember the last time I've seen Mom so lively. And Dad has a bounce in his step. He didn't look nearly as tired as usual, and he actually ran up the steps to put his laptop away. I can't remember the last time he willingly put that computer down. He's always either writing a story or researching for hints of Rachel.

Keith clearly liked Peter. He thought for sure the boy would choose to ride with him in the Mustang, but he hopped in Peter's Jeep. *What was it he said? I need to ride with Amber. Interesting statement. What is he—their chaperone or something? Maybe I've stepped into a time warp.*

Ryan pulled into the driveway and took his first good look at where his sister had been living the last couple of months. The beautiful log cabin sat peacefully on a small clearing surrounded by the forest. The windows shone brightly in the dimming light, and smoke curled out of the chimney. He turned off his engine and watched Sassy bound out of Peter's Jeep and into the garage with Keith right behind. *He feels at home here.*

Peter, Thomas, and Victoria followed Keith, but Amber stood waiting for him. "Ready to meet the in-laws?"

He smiled at her. "You're the one marrying into the family. I'm just tagging along for a bit. I can always leave if they're crazy."

She laughed. "They're definitely crazy. But in a good way. Consider yourself forewarned: Peter and his siblings are pranksters, taught by their grandfather." She turned to lead the way into the house.

"Does everyone still live in Crossing?"

"No, most of them live near Portland, but they come down a lot. His sister, Brittney, took off most of next week for the wedding, so you should meet her in a few days. Pops, the grandfather, normally travels down with her when she comes."

Amber opened the door into the mudroom, stomping her boots on the welcome mat. "You can hang your coat wherever you see space. And just put your boots on any of these shelves. Frank has a drain under this floor, so as the snow melts off of them, the water just drains back into the yard."

"Nice."

Sassy popped her head through the dog door and barked.

"We're coming, Sass."

Amber turned the knob and led Ryan into a casual dining area with French doors leading to a deck. His mom sat at a breakfast bar overlooking a spacious kitchen with his dad standing behind her. An older blonde woman hovered near the sink. *Five foot four, 160 pounds, mid-fifties. If the Pillsbury Doughboy were female*.... Ryan grinned at his assessment.

Both women turned to smile at them.

"You must be Ryan," said Faye. "Let me dry my hands."

She wiped her hands on a towel and came over to greet him. "It's so nice to finally have your whole family together." She gave Ryan a hug before wrapping an arm around Amber.

"Yes, ma'am," said Ryan. "You have a beautiful home."

"Why thank you, dear. How long do you get to stay?"

"A while."

Ryan caught his dad's quick glance in his direction.

"He needs a place to stay for a couple days while Mom and Dad get another room at Micah's cleaned out," said Amber. "I told him we had room here."

"Oh, absolutely," said Faye with a nod. "It's Peter's old room, and truthfully it's not completely cleaned out yet. He's taken most of his stuff to his new house, but he's not been gone that long, and I just haven't taken the time to clean it out properly. You are welcome to it if you'd like, though."

"Thank you."

"Don't let these women-folk push you into anything, young man."

An older man walked into the kitchen. *Just a bit taller than me, so five foot ten? His skin looks like he's used to working outside in the sun, and he's got some extra weight in the middle. What was the name of that '70s TV dad with all the kids where everyone said good night to everyone else?*

The man continued. "Sure enough, if you let them talk you into staying here, they'll fill you with good food all hours of the day and night. But this sister of yours'll roast you out of the living room stoking up the fire, and my wife'll have you tying up little satchels of good-smelling stuff for the wedding."

"Oh, Frank, really," said Faye, giggling.

Ryan watched his sister's smile grow. *She's happy here.*

"I'm Frank, by the way. Peter's dad." Frank extended his hand to Ryan.

"Nice to meet you, sir."

"So, when are y'all going to stop yammering around here and feed us?" said Frank to the women. "Lunch was a long time ago!"

"Just give us five more minutes," said Faye. "Amber, you go on in and show Ryan around while Victoria and I finish up the salad so we can eat."

Amber led Ryan into the living room where Keith and Peter sat over a chessboard.

"This is obviously the living room," said Amber. "And there's a library back here."

Ryan followed her behind a circular staircase to a small room covered in bookshelves. "That's an interesting picture."

Amber followed Ryan's gaze to a framed drawing of a maple tree sitting in front of a log cabin. In one top corner, a child's face smiled down on the scene.

"I drew that," said Amber.

"I remember you having a talent for drawing," said Ryan as he walked closer. "This is really good."

"Thanks."

"Is the child someone special?"

Amber looked at the child she'd sketched. "Her name is

Jamie. She was Peter's older sister."

"Was?"

"She died when she was ten." She looked at her brother.

He looked back at her, a lump forming in his throat. Returning his eyes to the picture, he said, "Have you made peace?"

"You mean with Cassie's death?"

Ryan nodded. "You were a lot closer to her than I was. I don't really have many memories of my oldest sister."

"You were only six when the accident happened, Ryan."

He looked back at his sister. "I remember one conversation we had shortly before you left. You said that you tried not to think about her because it hurt too much."

She sighed deeply. "Part of me still hurts, but I'm not angry anymore. I told God that I would rather have grown up with her, but ultimately I choose to trust Him and His choices."

She trusts God? Ryan's mind was tumbling again.

"Hey, Ray, Ryan," said Peter, coming around the corner to join them. "Mom's got dinner ready."

Ryan followed them back to the dining room and looked at the feast laid before him. The light blue tablecloth was barely noticeable underneath the dishes piled around the place setting for eight. Fried rice, Mexican corn, guacamole, refried beans, tortilla chips, and a huge salad surrounded two large dishes full of steamy melted cheese. It looked like a Mexican-themed Thanksgiving!

"Come on, everyone, before the enchiladas get cold," said Faye.

"Don't have to call me twice," said Thomas as he took a seat beside Frank.

Ryan hung back to see where everyone sat, watching Peter

hold out Amber's chair for her before sitting beside her.

"Ryan, come sit by your mother," said Faye with a smile and a pat on the back of the empty chair. Then she took her seat.

"All right now," said Frank. "Let's say grace."

Ryan watched Peter and his sister grab hands as they bowed their heads. *It seems natural, not awkward.*

"Thank you, Father, for this food smelling so good before us and adding yet another friend to our table. Let our conversation be good and keep us safe through the night. Amen."

"Now everyone eat up, but save room for dessert," said Faye. "I have caramel flan in the fridge for later."

"What's flan?" said Keith.

"It's a Mexican dessert, mostly sugar and sweetened milk," said Faye. "Peter, will you serve the enchiladas?"

"Sure," said Peter. "Let me see your plate, Mom."

As food began to be dished out, conversation began around the table as well.

"Your dad said you're a paramedic, Ryan," said Frank.

Ryan took the salad from his mom and added some to his bowl. "Yes, sir."

"Where do you work?" said Peter, handing a plate back to his mom and reaching for Ryan's.

"I'm down at McWilliam, just a couple hours west of here," said Ryan.

"Well that's not too far," said Faye.

"Mom said you were really busy at Christmas," said Amber.

"Yeah," said Ryan. "Besides my EMT job at the firehouse, I was pulling a bunch of extra hours at the hospital."

"Was that for a class you were taking?" Thomas asked, spooning some fried rice onto his plate.

"Kinda," said Ryan. "I was working with a couple of the doctors on diagnosis."

"Is that part of your training?" Peter asked as he added refried beans to his plate.

"Paramedics only have to have an associate's degree to get licensed. But I've been working toward getting my bachelor's."

"What are you going to do with that?" said Thomas.

Ryan clenched his jaw. "Not sure, Dad," said Ryan. He hated admitting that he wasn't sure what was driving him to complete more school, much less what he was going to do with it when he was done.

"Well, we're glad you're here now," said Faye.

Conversation turned to wedding planning and his dad's latest stories. Ryan relaxed a bit after the careful scrutiny on his job situation. *At least they didn't ask if I was considering moving again. I think I'll keep that to myself until I decide whether or not to move to a larger department in Portland.*

As the evening closed down, he knew he would have to make a decision about where he was sleeping. He'd rather just drive up the road toward Portland to find a hotel, but he didn't think that was going to fly.

His sister—maybe he would call her Rachel-Amber until he got used to using her middle name—slipped up to him and squeezed his arm. "I'd really like it if you'd stay here with us tonight, Ryan."

It seems a better option than Peter's. At least she is here, and I'm not forced into close quarters with the brother-in-law yet. "I guess the bride gets to decide," he said, smiling down at her. "I'll grab my bag."

Chapter 4

RYAN ROLLED OVER TO CHECK the time. *8:24. I suppose I should get up. Wonder what time they get moving around here.*

He grabbed clean jeans and a long sleeved T-shirt and headed to the shower. Ten minutes later, he walked down the stairs to find Rachel-Amber curled up on a chair by the fire reading.

"Morning."

"Morning, Ryan. Did you sleep okay?"

"Yeah."

"Frank and Faye are already gone, but there's fresh muffins in the kitchen if you're hungry."

"Got any coffee?"

"Let's go see." She sat her book aside and stood up, stretching her arms above her head before striking out for the kitchen. "Frank normally cleans it out before he leaves, but I can make some more."

Ryan watched her move around the kitchen. "You're really comfortable here."

She smiled as she poured water into the coffee maker. "Yes. When I first got here, I was a mess, but God brought me here where they just... I don't know. Enveloped me in love, I guess."

She emptied the coffee scoop into the filter and pushed the start button. "There, fresh coffee in just a few minutes."

"You know, I was mad at you for a long time." Ryan turned the basket of muffins around in his hands, focusing on the aroma wafting from the coffee maker rather than Rachel's face.

"Because I left?"

Ryan sighed deeply. "Because you left *me*."

"I'm sorry, Ryan."

He looked into her eyes for a moment, clenching his jaw. She offered no excuses for her behavior, just a simple apology. He wondered the same question that had haunted him for years: *Would I have done anything different if I'd been the older one?*

"I don't blame you, Rachel-Amber. It's really the catalyst that changed everything." Ryan paused, lost in thought. "Still, it was lonely without you."

"Do you think we can make up for it? I'm enjoying having Mom and Dad here. But I'd love it if you were around as well."

Ryan shrugged. "I don't know if I'm cut out to live in Mayberry."

She laughed. "I thought of Sheriff Taylor when I first got here too."

She filled a mug and handed it to him. "Milk, sugar?"

"Black is fine."

"Look, Ryan. I'm not asking you to *move* to Crossing. If you're happy in McWilliam, that's fine. It's not so far. Whatever town is best for you is okay by me. I'm just asking if maybe we can plan to spend more time together, get together on holidays, acknowledge birthdays, that kind of thing." Her voice trailed off as she waited for his response.

Ryan took a sip of coffee, thinking about all they had missed. *Not just the ten years she's been gone, but all the years before that were filled with misery.* "Maybe so."

He paused to look at her, squinting his left eye. "When's your birthday again?"

He waited to see how she'd react. Pain briefly reflected in her eyes. Until he smiled. Then he ducked as the kitchen towel came flying towards his face.

Ryan couldn't remember a better afternoon. Just relaxing with his sister and catching up on their lives soothed his spirit more than he'd thought possible. Now as they walked toward the logging office, memories came flooding back from a childhood summer camp.

"Remember that year Dad made us go to camp?"

Amber laughed. "The year they were infested with frogs?"

"We had to check the beds before we could go to sleep," said Ryan.

Amber opened the door to the office, stomping snow off her feet before entering. "And you took one home in your backpack!"

"Took one what?" said Faye, looking up from the small pile of orders in front of her.

"A frog," said Amber, giggling.

Ryan feigned innocence. "He was overcrowded in his home."

"Do I need to check your room?" said Faye, utterly confused.

Ryan's "No" met Amber's "Maybe," sending everyone laughing.

"Okay. I promise. No frogs," said Ryan, hands raised in surrender.

"Any other critters I should be worrying about?" asked Faye with raised eyebrows.

"I seem to remember..." said Amber.

Just then, a young man burst into the office. "Ms. Faye, have you got a rag or anythin' up here?"

Amber and Faye turned to see one of their employees, Chad Davis, holding his young son's nose, blood dripping from between his fingers. Amber immediately went for the first aid kit. Faye grabbed a roll of paper towels. Ryan knelt at the boy's side and tried to avoid the melting snow from his shoes.

"What happened?" asked Ryan.

"Nothin' I know of," said Chad. "It just started bleeding."

"Let me see a couple paper towels," said Ryan. He looked at the women. "Where can he sit?"

"Here." Amber rolled a chair over to Ryan.

Ryan gently took the paper towels and pinched the boy's nose right under his bridge. He placed his other hand behind the boy's head and leaned it forward slightly.

"Why don't you sit in the chair while I hold your nose, okay?" said Ryan. He glanced at his watch. "What's your name?"

"Josh."

"Well, Josh, it's nice to meet you. I'm Ryan."

Ryan felt Josh tremble.

"Bloody noses can be scary, but normally they're nothing to

worry about. Do you remember bumping your nose on anything, Josh?"

"No."

"How old are you?"

"Four."

Ryan looked at the boy sitting before him. *He's too calm.*
"Has this ever happened before?"

Josh nodded his head. Ryan looked at the man who brought
the boy here.

"Are you his father?"

"Yes. The name's Chad."

"How often does this happen?"

Chad spread his arms helplessly. "It started back a couple months
ago when he had the flu. He just ain't been the same since."

"Anyone else in the house sick?"

"No. Well, not really. My wife's been sick, but she's pregnant
and all, so it's not real sickness. Just because of the baby. And his
brother Caleb never got sick a'tall."

"Ryan?" Concern was evident in Amber's voice.

He shook his head. "It's most likely nothing. Sometimes kids
just get nosebleeds. Even the ones who tend to get them a lot
also tend to grow out of them."

He looked at young Josh. "I'm just going to hold on for
about another minute, then we'll see how it's doing, okay?"

Josh tried to nod his head, which was difficult since Ryan
had a grip on his nose.

Ryan turned his head and met Faye's anxious gaze. "He
might like something to drink. Sometimes a bit of the blood

will go down the throat."

Faye hurried to the small fridge they kept in the office.

"It don't taste good," said Josh, referring to the blood.

"No, it doesn't," Ryan agreed.

"If I remember…" said Faye. "Yes, I thought so." She came back with a small popsicle. "I thought Frank had some of these things down here last fall."

"Perfect," said Ryan. "Rachel-Amber, can you wet down a couple of paper towels for me?"

Ryan looked at Josh. "Okay, here's what we're going to do. I'm going to pull these paper towels on your nose away to see how we're doing. If it looks okay, then we'll use the wet ones to gently wipe around your nose. If it starts bleeding again, Mrs. Faye will have fresh paper towels ready for me, okay?"

Josh nodded his head. Faye grabbed a couple more paper towels off the roll as Amber walked up with some damp ones. Chad stood by his son, rubbing his back to comfort him.

Ryan put his free hand on Josh's shoulder. "Now, when you look down, you might see what looks like a lot of blood on these paper towels. Just remember that the body has lots of blood, and even though it looks like a lot on these towels, it's really not that bad, okay?"

Josh tried to nod again.

"Okay, let's take a look." Ryan gently pulled the towels away. "Looks good so far." After he dropped the bloody towels on the floor and grabbed the wet towels from Amber, Ryan gently began to clean the stained and crusted area around Josh's nose and mouth.

"There," said Ryan, sitting back on his heels and looking Josh in the eye. "That looks better. Ready for your popsicle?"

As he stood, he wrapped the bloody towels in the clean ones and turned to Chad. Speaking quietly, he said, "Why don't we go wash our hands?"

Chad looked at him for a moment and then looked down at his own blood-covered hands. "Oh. Yeah. Good idea."

As the women fussed over Josh, Chad and Ryan walked to the bathroom.

"Thank you," said Chad.

"Any time," said Ryan.

"You seem to know a lot about all that. You think it's serious?"

Ryan looked back toward the little boy; Josh was swinging his legs, totally content with his treat. "You said he hasn't been quite right since the flu a couple months ago. What else is different?"

"Well, he's been quieter than normal. Don't want to go out so much like he used to. Then there's the nosebleeds. Like I said. He seems to get 'em all the time."

"How many?"

"To be honest, I lost count. Seems like they come about every other day or so."

Ryan looked at Chad. "I'm no doctor, sir, just a paramedic. But I'd recommend a visit to his doctor. Just to be safe."

Chapter 5

AS CHAD AND LITTLE JOSH left the logging office, two flaxen-haired men dressed in blue jeans and winter coats watched from the edge of the woods.

"Things are coming together nicely," said Matthew.

"So far," said Michael as a ruby-crowned kinglet landed on his shoulder.

"You still have doubts?"

The bird flicked its wings, and Michael reached up to take the bird in his hands. "What's the saying? Don't count your chickens before they're hatched?"

"Yes, but this family has a strong influence."

"True."

A second kinglet lighted on the branch above Matthew, dropping bits of snow onto his curly head. He brushed it off absently with his bare hand. "But doubts remain?"

"Yes. Try not to underestimate the enemy," said Michael. "He is very powerful. And motivated."

"I still believe in this family."

"Good. But don't let your guard down."

Chapter 6

RYAN WATCHED HIS SISTER PERIODICALLY throughout the Sunday morning church service. Sitting next to Peter in her khaki pants and sweater, she held her own Bible and followed along with the pastor. *She seems to be comfortable here, too.*

Religion confused Ryan. He believed in both God and the Bible, but past that, it got complicated. *Jesus rose from the dead. Why can't church be that simple?*

As the music ended and the family prepared to leave, several well-wishers crowded around to meet him and talk about the wedding happening in just six days. Yes, he was glad to have his sister back in his life. Yes, he was excited for her to be marrying Peter. *Really, how else do these people expect me to answer these questions? Of course I'm happy for her, but I don't really know Peter or his family.*

Finally Peter politely excused them and led Amber and Ryan down the aisle and outside the church.

"Is the whole town invited to the wedding?" asked Ryan, slipping his arms into his coat.

Amber giggled. "Seems like it."

"I believe Mom did invite everyone at church," Peter said almost apologetically.

"And our mother has been inviting everyone who walks into the hardware store for the last three weeks." Humor sparkled in Amber's eyes.

"Awesome." Ryan's voice sounded strained. He tugged his tie loose before zipping up his coat.

"My thoughts exactly," said Peter.

Amber looked from her future husband to her brother as she snuggled further into her coat. "You two." She rolled her eyes. "At least you won't be the one in a dress!"

"And that's a good thing, my Ray," said Peter.

"By the way, who is Mrs. Guire?" asked Ryan.

"Why?" said Amber. "Where'd you meet her?"

"Inside. She was asking me all about my car. Some of the questions I'm used to, like what year it is. But other questions were strange."

"Like what?" Peter asked.

"She asked me if I'd upgraded the steering to rack and pinion! How many old ladies ask that question?"

Amber laughed. "That makes sense."

"Yeah," said Peter. "You have to know her. Some places have a town drunk or town black sheep. We have a town hot-rodder. And it's not any of the teenage boys."

"Her?" said Ryan. "You've got to be kidding me! She's got to be sixty years old."

"Yep," said Amber, nodding. "Sixty-three and a constant blip on Sheriff Daniel's radar. Plus she owns the small garage in town.

Worked around cars all her life from what I can tell."

Ryan shook his head. *Sixty-three. Probably not five feet tall stretched out or one hundred pounds fully dressed. That woman must have a great story. What old woman asks about a gearbox?*

"Wasn't that a nice service?" said Thomas, walking up behind his daughter and putting an arm around her shoulders.

"Do you have plans for lunch?" Victoria had arrived behind Thomas and was now looking at Ryan.

"I'm open to whatever," said Ryan.

Amber reached out to touch her mother's arm. "Logan and Heather will be coming down later today, Mom. Want to come over?"

"Logan and Heather?" said Ryan.

"Peter's older brother and his wife," Amber explained.

"Oh good, Amber dear," said Faye, joining the small group. "I'm glad you invited everyone. I would have called you, Victoria, but Logan didn't let us know until this morning. He said they would be here around 3:00 and will spend the night with Peter. You are welcome to come over whenever you'd like. Tomorrow too. We'll be going over all the lists to make sure everything is planned for."

"Dinner sounds wonderful," said Thomas. "But I think I'll skip the lists."

"Can we bring anything?" said Victoria.

"I think I'll skip the lists with you," said Peter with a wink at his soon-to-be father-in-law.

"To keep things simple," said Faye, "I think I'll just make some ham and potato soup with grilled cheese sandwiches."

"Can I skip the lists?" said Amber with a mischievous grin.

"How about I bring some brownies?" said Victoria, ignoring the silliness around her.

"I know I'm skipping the lists," said Ryan.

"Perfect!" said Faye. "The girls will love that!"

"Girls?" said Ryan.

"My brother has three girls," Peter explained. "A four-year old, two-year old, and an infant."

Ryan nodded his head. *It doesn't sound like the afternoon will be peaceful. Maybe it would be a good afternoon to head to Portland.*

"And by the way, Peter dear," said Faye with a look.

"Yes, Mom?"

"Amber will need you by her side as we go over the lists," said Faye.

Ryan chuckled as Peter groaned.

"Yes," said Victoria, "and I think we should assign a few things to Ryan, as well."

"Me?" Ryan putted his hands up to his chest looking from his mom to Faye. Both women's eyes were sparkling. *I'm not getting out of this one easily.*

"Misery does love company, son," said Thomas.

"Yes, it does," said Victoria. "And if you want any potato soup, my dear husband, I suggest you look over the lists and find a job or two for which you are willing to be responsible."

"Me?" said Thomas. He looked at his wife then sighed deeply.

Ryan smirked at his dad and then shrugged. "Looks like we've been busted."

"Well," said Peter, "let's get some lunch so we have strength to face the inevitable."

※※※※※※※※

Ryan found his sister five hours later on the back deck of the Yager home. "Escaping lists?"

She turned to look at him, smiling. "Yeah."

"I'm with you! Where do we abandon ship?"

She laughed. "Did you get your assignments?"

"Unfortunately. I thought I was just attending this shindig. Somehow my plan went terribly wrong!"

She laughed again. "Just wait until Brittney gets here."

"Who is Brittney again?"

"She's Peter's sister, and she's a ball of energy. She'll have us all completing our lists in record time."

"Maybe we could trade assignments. Who has the easy job?"

"Baby Megan!"

"Think she'll trade me?"

She laughed. "Thanks. I needed to refocus, and you helped."

"What's the problem?"

"Oh, just too many details to think about. I don't really care where people sit or how much food we buy, whether everyone throws rice or blows bubbles. I just want to be Peter's wife."

"Why does he call you Ray when everyone else calls you Amber? Is it short for Rachel?"

She turned to look at him. "I suppose it could be, but that's not where he got it. It's what my initials will be after we're married: R-A-Y."

"That's kinda corny."

She smiled back at his grin. "Yeah, it is. But I love it."

He shook his head. "Women."

"What?!"

"You get all mushy at some of the silliest things."

"True. Have you never had anyone special, Ryan?"

Ryan shrugged. "Nah."

"Why not?"

He turned to look towards the woods behind the house, the snow glistening on the trees. "Truth be told, I move around a lot."

"What do you mean?"

"I stay at a job for six or eight months, get restless, and move on."

"Move on to another department, or another town?"

"Town, mostly."

"What about friends?"

Ryan shrugged as he gazed at the woods without seeing them. "I hang out with some of the guys I work with, but I've really only had one good friend in the last several years. We went to high school together."

"Where's he now?"

"He joined the Army shortly after we graduated. Got assigned to Ft. Lewis near Tacoma. We used to see each other two or three times a year, but his deployments make it hard. Life moves on and all that."

"Oh, Ryan."

He turned to look at her, seeing concern in her eyes. "It's not a big deal."

"You're running, Ryan."

"You're crazy. What would I be running from?"

"Life."

Such a little word. Ryan clenched his jaw and turned back to the trees. He wanted to laugh at her, tell her she was wrong, but something held him back.

You are a great warrior.

Ryan almost laughed at the ridiculous words. *Where'd that come from?* Maybe this fresh mountain air was getting to him.

"Aunt Am-er!" Two-year old Taylor came running onto the deck.

Ryan watched his sister scoop the blonde cutie into her arms.

"Taylor, what are you doing out here without shoes on?"

"You play Candyland wit' me?"

"Are your sister and Uncle Peter done with their game?"

"Uncle Pe-er says it your turn now."

"Okay, sweetie." Amber looked at Ryan.

"If nothing's going on the next couple of days," said Ryan, "I think I'll head into Portland and look around."

Amber looked at him steadily then nodded her head. He felt like she was seeing through him. *Maybe we're more alike than I'm ready to admit.*

"You play Candyland?" said Taylor, looking at Ryan.

He looked into her big blue eyes. "Only if I can be the green man."

She smiled back at him. "Am-er like the boo man. I be lell-lo, okay?"

Chapter 7

"ALL RIGHT," SAID NICOLE. "I'LL take it from here."

Brittney looked at the nurse who was taking over the night shift in the oncology unit at Doernbecher Children's Hospital. "It seems like I'm forgetting something."

"We've got it, Britt. Go enjoy your family. We'll see you next week."

"Okay. I'm going to say bye to Grace first."

Brittney looked in the window before tying the fibrous isolation gown around her slim waist and putting on the gloves. The gentle five-year-old lay quietly in bed, cartoons flickering across her television screen. It didn't seem like that long ago when a vibrant girl with long blonde curls had come bouncing onto the ward.

After tying the mask strings around her long, dark hair that was pulled back into a ponytail, Brittney opened the door and stepped inside. "Hey, Gracie."

A smile appeared on the little girl's face. "Hi, B. Is it time for you to leave?"

Brittney walked over to the bed. "Yes. Nicole is here and will be in to see you in a little bit." She watched the child breathe.

"Will you bring me a picture of you all dressed up for the wedding?"

"If you want." Brittney straightened out a couple lines running from the fragile child to the machines keeping tabs on her vitals. "But you have to promise me you'll be really good while I'm gone and do everything Nicole asks you to do."

"Okay."

Brittney glanced up at the monitor. *Her O2 sats are lower than they were this morning.* Brittney's training reminded her that low oxygen saturation or O2 sats, as it was commonly called, affected the ability of the oxygen to get into the red blood cells. Over time, Grace's heart and other organs would be weakened.

"I'll be back to work next Tuesday."

"I'll miss you, B."

Brittney tried to swallow the lump in her throat, gently touching the child's shoulder. "I'll miss you, too, Gracie."

She walked out, cast off her isolation gear and went back to the nurse's station. "Nicole."

Nicole looked up from checking her watch. "Yeah, Britt."

"Her O2 sats are down a bit from this morning."

"Okay. I'll keep an eye on her."

"Nicole." Brittney paused.

"I got her, Britt." Nicole walked over and placed an understanding hand on Brittney's arm. "I'll call you if she heads downhill. Promise."

Brittney fought the tears striving to roll down her cheeks. "Thanks." She cleared her throat and said, "I'll see you next week."

In the locker room she struggled to maintain her composure. As she traded her scrubs for jeans and a sweatshirt, her mind circled around Gracie's latest test results. *Stage IV. Results indicate non-Hodgkin lymphoma has spread in patient's abdomen to include the intestines, colon, and spleen. Further tests show evidence of cancer cells in the blood and cerebrospinal fluid.*

Oh, Daddy. Brittney sat down on the bench, covering her face with her hands as she prayed. *Father, I know you are the Great Physician. If I could save any child, it would be Gracie. But more than her healing, I want Your best. Father, help me accept whatever that is, whatever that looks like. And cover Gracie with Your love while I'm gone. Please, Daddy, do not let her die alone.*

She sat for a few minutes before grabbing her purse and heading to the elevators. She needed a hot bath and a good night's sleep before she picked up Pops for the drive to wedding headquarters. *And maybe a pint of Tillamook's mint chocolate chip ice cream.*

✻✻✻✻✻✻✻✻✻✻✻✻✻✻

"Hey, Mom!" Brittney stomped her snow-covered boots on the rough mat and closed the office door behind her. "Hey, Amber. I brought a treat!"

"What did you bring?" said Faye from her desk to the left of the door.

As if it were a trophy, Brittney held up a white bag featuring the logo of Romano's Macaroni Grill. "Lemon passion cake from Romano's."

"Yes!" said Amber, slamming the file cabinet shut and walking over to join Brittney at Faye's desk.

"Oh, that sounds delicious," said Faye. "Where's Pops?"

Brittney opened the bag and pulled out portions of the cake and three plastic forks. "He headed down to the shop to see if he could find any of the men-folk."

Amber accepted the boxed slice of cake. Walking over to her own desk opposite Faye's, she opened the box, smiled, and used the plastic fork to help herself to a taste. "Hmmm. This is really good," said Amber. "Thanks!"

"You look tired," said Faye, taking a bite of her own slice of cake.

"I am," said Brittney. She lowered herself into a chair beside Faye's desk. "One of my kids isn't doing so well."

"I'm sorry, dear," said Faye. "How are the parents taking it?"

Brittney rolled her eyes. "Who knows? They're at the Ronald McDonald House but rarely darken the oncology doors."

"Why wouldn't they be with their child?" said Amber, aghast.

"Sometimes parents are too selfish to spend much time on the ward. They find any excuse to leave because they can't take the boredom of sitting in a hospital room. Sometimes they have other responsibilities, like jobs or children that make it difficult to stay for long periods of time. Some parents just find their child's illness inconvenient to their own schedules."

"But you don't think these parents fall into any of those categories," said Faye with knowing eyes.

"No, Mom, I don't." Brittney put her plate down on Faye's desk. "I think these parents are just weak. When they come to visit, they want to spend all their time at the nurse's station. When they do enter their daughter's room, they act like they're afraid to go anywhere near her. And when they leave, they can't quit apologizing."

"You, my dear, spend every day dealing with cancer," said Faye. "Some people are intimidated by the machines and equipment you work with all the time."

"I know, Mom. And I try to offer grace for that. But I watch them show up and leave within just thirty minutes almost every day. The mother especially seems burdened with guilt. And in the meantime, this five year old lays in a hospital bed twenty-four hours a day, alone."

Amber paused with her fork in mid-air. "It sounds like this particular five year old means something to you."

Brittney sighed, her eyes filling with tears. "Her name is Grace. Before chemo, she had blonde curls down her back and so much energy we had trouble keeping her in bed."

"How bad is it now?" said Faye.

"Pretty bad, Mom. She has lymphoma, and it's passed to her blood supply. The lab thinks it's spread throughout her abdomen and into her spinal cord."

"Brittney, we would love for you to participate in our wedding," said Amber, "but don't let us keep you from Grace. If you need to be there, then go."

Brittney smiled. "Thanks. But she's in good hands. Nicole said she'd call if things get worse. And I can't do a thing for her that the nurses there aren't already doing." Brittney paused to look at Amber. "It's another trust issue, right?"

"Right," said Amber, pointing her fork at Brittney. "Do you trust God to take care of Grace or not?"

"Right," said Brittney. She took a deep breath. "So, what's going on around here? Catch me up on all the wedding news."

"How 'bout we close up this office early and head back to the house?" said Faye, putting her cake down and grabbing a tissue for her eyes.

"Who's closing up early?" Peter stomped his boots and entered, leaving the door open for Ryan behind him. Upon closing the door, both men froze.

"Uh-oh," said Peter. "Three women. All in tears. Open plates of half-eaten cake. Hormones must be in overdrive."

"Hey!" said Brittney and Amber.

"Shall I sound a retreat?" said Ryan.

"To the grocery store for ice cream," said Peter.

"Already got it in the car," said Brittney, looking up at the stranger beside her brother.

"You brought it with you?" said Peter. "This is serious!"

"You can't even imagine!" Not wanting to talk about Grace any more, Brittney feigned great drama. Throwing a hand to her forehead, effectively hiding the dampness around her eyes, she said, "I broke a nail!" She held her other hand out toward the guys.

"Please!" said Peter, throwing a glove at her face.

"Sweet! I needed a new glove," said Brittney, catching it.

With thoughts of the sick child effectively removed, Faye giggled. "You two. Are any of you children going to remember your manners and introduce Ryan?"

"This is your brother?" said Brittney.

"Yeah," said Amber. "But watch it. He and Peter are getting

along very well." She looked at Brittney, raising one eyebrow.

"Are they now?" said Brittney, eying him appraisingly. "And has he been warned?"

"Warned about what?" said Ryan.

"Brittney, what are you thinking?" said Faye.

"Britt," said Peter.

Amber giggled.

"Well, I'm just saying," said Brittney in all innocence. "If the men-folk are getting along so nicely…"

"Britt," said Peter with a warning in his tone.

Brittney stood and faced her brother. "Yes, my dear Peter?"

"Uh, Ryan?" said Peter. "Remember that retreat you were talking about?"

"Yeah," said Ryan.

"Now might be a good time," said Peter.

"Uh-huh," said Ryan. "Well, ladies, it was good to see you. Nice to meet you, Brittney. But we must be gettin' along. We have…uh…lists…"

"Logs…" said Peter.

"Logs… to uh, count," said Ryan.

"Cut," said Peter.

"Right. Cut," said Ryan.

As both men backed out of the logging office, the ladies broke out in laughter.

"Brittney, dear. What are you thinking?" said Faye.

"Amber," said Brittney, "how many pranks did your family pull growing up?"

"None," said Amber.

"Perfect," said Brittney. "Why don't we…"

"Stop right there," said Faye. "You guys have your fun, but leave my ears out of this so's I can't be sweet talked out of any information!"

Chapter 8

RYAN PULLED INTO THE DRIVEWAY and saw Rachel-Amber's soon-to-be sister-in-law sitting on the porch swing. He parked and walked over to her.

"Kinda cold for sitting outside, isn't it?"

"Most of the time," said Brittney. Her warm breath turned to fog in the chilled air.

"Only most?"

"I needed to be outside for a bit but didn't feel like going for a walk on my own."

"Would you rather be alone sitting here?" said Ryan.

"No. Do you mind sitting for a bit?"

"You're not going to have me sit in a pile of superglue or something?"

She smiled mischievously but shook her head. "Peter's been talking, huh?"

"Between the stories he and Pops shared Sunday, I'm glad I went ahead and moved to town to stay with my parents above the hardware store!"

"Chicken."

He grinned. Brittney may be two or three inches shorter than him and not any bigger around than his skinny sister, but her spunk appealed to him. "You don't back down from a fight, do you?"

"Not if it's worth fighting."

A glint of determination in her eyes caught his attention. "What do you do for a living?"

"I'm a nurse."

"In Portland?"

"Yeah. Doernbecher Children's Hospital."

"You work with kids?" That appealed to Ryan, who also had a soft spot where children were concerned. "What ward?"

She pulled her legs up and wrapped her arms around them. "Oncology." Her voice was low.

"Whoa. You are a fighter." Giving the seat a quick glance, he finally sat down beside her. Something in her pose, the defensive movement of pulling her legs against her, pulled at Ryan's protective instincts.

"Sometimes the battle makes you weary," she said.

"You got a kid having a rough time?"

"Yeah."

Her look seemed distant, like she was at the hospital. *She cares deeply.* Ryan turned slightly sideways in the porch swing, laying his arm along the back. His fingers brushed her shoulder.

Brittney blinked and looked at him. "What about you? What do you do?"

"Paramedic."

"Really? Where at?"

"I'm down in McWilliam, but I don't know how long I'm staying there."

"How come?"

Ryan clenched his jaw for a moment and stared across the front yard. "It just doesn't feel like the right place. My boss is great, and the guys I work with are fine." Ryan paused. "I don't know. Mom says I'm restless. Maybe she's right."

"Are you sure being a paramedic is the right job?"

"I love the job, or at least most of it. I don't think I could deal with floor duty in a hospital."

"Being a paramedic certainly has a rush that's not as common as where I work. But what about the ER? That's more high activity."

"Yeah, but I don't think so."

"Is it the people?"

He turned to look at her. "The patients?"

"Well, them, too," said Brittney. "But first I guess you need to decide if you like working with just a few people, like you do in the ambulance, or a lot of people like you'd encounter at a hospital. I don't mind a lot of people, but when I work, I'd rather just focus on a few. I'd rather develop relationships so I can see the nuances that sometimes make the difference in diagnosis and treatment."

"Guess I've never thought about that before." Ryan sat back.

"Not sure it helps you figure out what to do with the job in McWilliam, but it might help you narrow the possibilities."

"Especially if I head into Portland."

"Portland?" Brittany looked at him more closely. "Thinking

about moving closer to your family?"

Ryan shrugged noncommittally. "Just a thought."

Ryan heard an engine behind him. He and Brittney both turned to watch a black Camry pulling into the drive.

"There's Mom and Amber. Want to go inside for some coffee?"

The car drove around to the three-car garage on the far side of the house. Ryan heard the garage door opening.

"Can I ask you a question? I've noticed that Peter and Amber are rarely alone, especially in a car or building. And now I'm guessing that you kept me out here until someone else showed up. Why is that?"

"Most people think it's a bit old-fashioned, but it's all about accountability. We try hard not to be alone in a private space with someone of the opposite gender that we're not related or married to. Just keeps everyone safe from accusations and misunderstandings."

Ryan's mind reeled. Were these people seriously living by standards of the 1950s? "So you wouldn't get into a car alone with me to drive to town."

"Not unless it was an emergency."

"And Peter and Amber won't drive alone until they are married?"

"Yep."

"But they're getting married in a couple of days."

"No. They are *planning* on getting married in a couple days. What if something happens, and the wedding gets canceled? What if one of them isn't as sure as we think they are and backs out? If they've already crossed the line the Bible places on single people, thinking it's okay because the wedding date is set, do you see the mess that would create if plans changed?"

"Interesting." He stood and looked at her. "It's a tough standard to maintain these days." He reached out a hand, helping her out of the swing.

"Yes, tough. But not impossible. Especially when family and friends understand that you are trying to honor God's Word. They've got lots of support and people willing to step in and chaperone as needed."

Faye opened the front door. "Are you two going to continue to freeze on the front porch, or can I interest you in some hot chocolate?"

"Sounds good, Mom," said Brittney.

"Got any coffee?" said Ryan.

Ryan stood back to allow Brittney to enter the house before him. He looked down at his hand, keenly aware of her touch when he had helped her up from the swing.

Peter got everyone's attention. "I won't take long because we all know the women have this better organized than I ever could. Amber and I just want to take this moment to thank everyone for coming out tonight and for everything I know you'll be doing the next couple of days. Your friendship and support multiply the blessings of this weekend.

"I can't imagine my life without any of you," Peter paused to look around the room. "You've always been there to guide me, watch over me, and sometimes let me fall. But with each failure, you lovingly helped me get back up and get moving in the right direction again."

"You done with the mushy stuff yet?" said Pops.

Ryan smiled. The old man was rough around the edges, but his love for his family was clear. And it was clear that he considered Amber family.

"Heather, it's all yours," said Peter, sitting down on the hearth beside Amber.

"Now don't take too long," said Thomas. "There's cobbler in the kitchen!"

As Heather began listing the details of what needed to be done when and what time everyone was supposed to be at different places, Ryan looked at the people gathered in Frank and Faye's living room. His sister was right. This family was different from any he'd been around before.

Peter, Logan, and Brittney were close as siblings, and Logan's wife and kids enhanced the relationships. If he didn't know better, he'd swear Micah's son, Andy, and Andy's wife, Allie, were part of the blood relatives somehow. And even now, watching them interact, Keith was being drawn into the mix like he belonged. *Bringing an outsider into the midst of this family bonds them closer together.*

Do you want to be included, great warrior?

The question took Ryan by surprise, and he wasn't sure how to answer. *Of course I want to be included, but I'm not sure I'm ready for what that means. Could I let myself be included? Rachel found her peace here as Amber; she was able to brave the risk to let people get close. Mom and Dad are definitely different. Dad's not been bugging me about moving or spending time with them like he used to do. It's been…nice.*

Ryan was shocked at his own assessment. His parents were changing, but whether that was due to finding their long-lost daughter or this family, he wasn't sure.

What about you, great warrior?

Ryan looked around the room. The voice was so audible, yet he was certain no one around him had said anything. *And what is this 'great warrior' thing?*

Silence.

Great. Best case, I'm talking to myself; worst case, I'm hearing voices.

"Is that okay with you, Ryan?" said Heather.

"Huh? Sorry. My mind wandered for a minute," said Ryan.

"Can you go with Logan to pick up all the tuxes in the morning?" said Heather. "You can take care of your final fitting then."

"Sure," said Ryan. "Whatever you need."

"I think that's it," said Heather.

"Okay," said Andy. "Just to be sure, tomorrow we meet at the church at noon to decorate, then at five for rehearsal. Saturday morning, the girls meet at the church by noon for pictures, guys at one, and doors open to guests at 1:30."

"Yes," said Brittney.

"You got it," said Allie. "Except you forgot the whole part where you turn off your phone and ignore Mrs. Guire's calls for the next two days."

Everyone laughed.

"Can we eat the cobbler now?" said Thomas.

"One more thing," said Peter. He turned to Brittney, and she handed him a red jeweler's case. "Thanks, Britt." He turned to look at Amber. "This is for the newest Mrs. Yager to wear on her wedding day. Brittney promises it matches your dress."

Amber opened the box and gasped, putting one hand to her mouth. "Oh, Peter. It's beautiful." She turned the case to show the zigzag necklace and earring set made with pearls. "Thank you."

He took her hand in his. "You are welcome, Ray."

"More mush," said Pops, shaking his head. "Weddings must turn his brain soft." He turned to Faye. "What kind of cobbler you got in there, Faye? Blackberry?"

Ryan watched Amber and Peter talking softly. She was going to be just fine.

And you, great warrior?

Chapter 9

BRITTNEY SLIPPED INTO A CLASSROOM at the church and looked at the row of dresses hanging neatly along the coat rack on the wall. She hadn't seen so much chiffon and satin since Logan's wedding. She fingered the fine material and let it slip through her fingers.

"Tomorrow will be beautiful," said Faye, walking in and hugging Brittney close.

"Yes, it will." She paused then said, "Do you think about Jamie when we have family events like this, Mom?"

Faye sighed. "Yes. I imagine the woman she would have become, wonder how her being here would have changed the dynamic between you and your brothers."

"Things would have been more fair growing up!"

Faye giggled. "Yes, perhaps so. The two of you could have teamed up on them—not that you normally needed a lot of help from anyone. Why do you ask?"

Brittney sighed. "I love Heather dearly, and can't imagine life without Allie. Now Amber's joining the family, and I'm really thankful for her. But, it's times like this that I most wonder about Jamie."

"Events like this would have suited her quite well."

"She was the one who loved to dress up and have tea parties."

Faye smiled. "Yes, she did. But then, by now she might have been married and moved to the other side of the country. You just never know."

Brittney's thoughts turned to Melody, the unit secretary at work who was waiting to marry her prince. He was on active duty in the military, and Brittney knew that Melody sometimes wondered if she was cut out to be an Army wife.

"Well, at least I'm not the only girl anymore. And both my brothers have found women that fit well into the family."

"God definitely gave me a 'Yes' answer to my prayers about the boys' wives." Faye looked at Brittney, placing a hand on her cheek. "And I know God will provide you with a man whom we will love too."

"Thanks, Mom. I'm glad you've prayed for him all my life."

"Mind if I interrupt?" said Amber, stepping into the room.

"Of course not, dear," said Faye, turning toward her.

"I just don't know what to do with myself," said Amber, spreading her arms wide. "Everything seems to be ready. I've adjusted the bows so many times they are starting to show wear, and I can tell you it's exactly twenty-eight steps from the back door to the front altar."

Faye laughed and wrapped her arm around Amber's shoulders.

"Well, since we have to fit into all these dresses tomorrow, gorging on ice cream is out of the question," said Brittney.

Amber and Faye both laughed.

"I just need to busy my mind for a while," said Amber.

"We could go back to the house and play a game or work a puzzle… or, we could start addressing thank you cards," said Brittney with a big smile.

"That sounds like a great time," said Amber as she rolled her eyes.

Brittney looked at her mom. "She's getting this sarcasm thing pretty good."

Amber laughed.

"Come on, my girls," said Faye. "You can decide what you want to do on the drive back to the house."

Brittney pulled out a deck of cards and drew Logan, Heather, Victoria, Keith, and Ryan into a game with her and Amber while Faye occupied Emma and Taylor with a princess movie. The house quickly filled with laughter and sibling rivalry that had little Emma looking at them and asking Faye if everyone was "playing nice."

"Anyone want more to drink?" asked Ryan, rising to his feet with his own empty glass.

"I'll take some more lemonade," said his mother.

"Me too," said Keith.

"I just want some water," said Amber.

"I'll help you, Ryan," said Brittney, pushing back from the table.

Brittney grabbed the glasses Ryan couldn't carry and headed into the kitchen behind him.

"I've been thinking about what you said." Ryan began to refill the water glasses.

"About what?" said Brittney as she sat the glasses she held on the counter.

"Career options."

"And…"

"And I like the idea of forming relationships with people, but I'm not sure I'm cut out for that."

"If you like the idea, then what's the problem?" Brittney grabbed the lemonade out of the fridge.

"I don't know if it will make any sense to you."

"Try it."

"I don't know how much you know about our past." Ryan grabbed the rag from the sink and began cleaning water droplets from the counter.

Brittney tried to hang back, let him share whatever he was comfortable with, but something in her yearned to know more. *What keeps him running from friendships? The death of his sister sixteen years before? Amber running away ten years ago? Something else?* "Amber's told me quite a lot."

"Well, I've looked at my work history and figured out that I choose to move on about the time that my partners start insisting on knowing more about me. The first few weeks, I can give them partial answers or divert the subject, and they're fine. But after three or four months, that's not good enough anymore."

"Are you scared to let people in?"

Ryan shrugged. "Yeah, I guess so. Well, not *scared,* but... I mean, how do I know they're dependable?" He stopped and gave an almost imperceptible shake of his head. "That's not quite right. I know I can depend on them to get the job done, but..." Ryan clenched his jaw.

Brittney walked over and stood right in front of him. She wanted to reach out to him, to touch his arm, but settled for reaching out with her words instead. "But, what?"

"Maybe I don't know what I'm missing, what I'm looking for."

"I know Amber struggled with learning to depend on people, wondering if Peter and the rest of us were going to abandon her tomorrow, not knowing whether she'd be okay if something happened to one of us," said Brittney.

She saw something flicker through his expression but wasn't sure what to make of it. The phone rang, interrupting her concentration.

She picked up the glasses he'd refilled and started to head back to the living room. "You can choose to consider the positive side of things too, Ryan. What if your partner or whatever person who wants to know more about you is here tomorrow?"

"Hey, Britt," said Logan. "The phone's for you."

"Thanks." She put the glasses down, turned to the wall by the breakfast bar and reached for the handset.

"Hello?"

"Hey, Brittney. It's Nicole."

Brittney's heart froze. She closed her eyes and forced herself to breathe. Her voice barely cooperated. "What's up?"

"Grace is still hanging in there, but her O2 stats are a bit lower, and her heart rate's dropped a few beats."

"What's she reading?"

"The O2's been hovering around 87 today, and the heart rate keeps dipping below 80."

"How's her breathing?"

"It's more steady than not, but there's some wheezing, and at times it gets shallow or ragged."

Brittney sighed deeply. The child's body was slowly being deprived of oxygen. How long could it hold out?

"There's more, Britt. The parents came in today and talked to the doctors for a while. Before they left, they signed a DNR."

Brittney sank down onto the barstool. *A Do Not Resuscitate order? Oh, Daddy.* Her heart cried out to God even as her mind ran through what she knew was the medical reality. Gracie's body could not handle much more.

She sighed deeply. "Okay. Thanks for calling."

"Melissa's got the night shift for the next two nights and Diane the next three days. Both know to call you if it gets critical."

"Thanks, Nicole."

Brittney heard the line click off, but she just couldn't quite make her muscles work to return the phone to its cradle. She felt Ryan beside her, gently taking the phone from her hand. He sat beside her, putting a hand on the middle of her back.

"Your kid?"

Brittney nodded, struggling to control her emotions. "She's dying."

"Is there no hope?"

"Little." Brittney sighed again and wiped the tears from her eyes.

"How long?"

"A week. Maybe more. Probably less."

"So now what?"

Brittney took a deep breath. "She's in good hands. I trust the ladies I work with, and I know the women assigned to her. They'll call me if…" Brittney closed her eyes. "They'll call me when she gets critical," she finally managed to whisper.

"And then we'll make sure you get the hospital," said Ryan reassuringly.

"Even if it's during the wedding," said Amber, stepping forward from the doorway.

"Amber," said Brittney in an attempt to object.

"No, Brittney," said Amber. "We both know that little girl will need you. You keep your cell phone close, and someone will be ready to get you to Portland if the need arises."

"Hey, if it gets me out of a tux…" said Logan.

Heather slapped Logan on the arm; his attempt at humor fell flat. This was no laughing matter.

Brittney smiled gratefully, looking at the collection of concerned family members gathered in the kitchen. "Thanks, everyone. I really appreciate it."

Chapter 10

THE AFTERNOON SUN REFLECTED OFF the snow-covered lawn. Michael stood tall at the roadside, looking toward the house. "The enemy will soon make himself a nuisance. Is the man ready?"

"Almost, sir," said Matthew. "Ryan's made great progress these past few days. He's letting Brittney in and renewing relationships with his family. I will make a visit to see him in the morning and plant the final seeds of courage."

"Good. He will need it. Do you still believe he will stay?"

"Yes. His heart draws him, although he does not yet acknowledge it."

"But will it be enough?"

Matthew reached out to pet the brown neck of an elk that had wandered close. Two other elk stood nearby, gnawing on white aspen trunks. "Men have done more with less."

Michael looked directly at Matthew. "And men with more have run."

"Yes. But I still believe he will stay."

Chapter II

THE ROOM GREW BRIGHT, LIKE the sun decided to rest on the bookshelf near Ryan's door. He squinted and rolled over to see a man standing there. Casually dressed in blue jeans and hiking boots, his pale hair and blue eyes commanded attention.

"The Lord is with you, great warrior."

"What? Who are you?"

"My name is Matthew."

"What do you want?"

"I've come to tell you that you are being sent, great warrior."

"Sent?" Ryan sat up in bed, rubbed his face, and ran his hands through his hair. "Who's sending me?"

"The Father."

Ryan looked at the man in disbelief. "The Father."

"Yes."

Matthew looked steadily upon him.

The man appears to be sincere, but how did he get in my room? And... is he supposed to be an angel? Ryan turned to look at the clock on the nightstand. It read 6:17am. *It's too early for anyone to be up. It's even too early for the sun to be up!*

"So, where am I supposed to go?"

"Being sent does not necessarily mean a change in location. Sometimes it simply refers to a destination."

Ryan shook his head. "Okay, I've not had my caffeine yet this morning. Do you have to speak in riddles?"

"A challenge is before you, great warrior. You were made for more than you've taken hold of. Go in the strength you have, but remember Who sends you. Do not be afraid."

Ryan rubbed his face again. "How do I know this isn't just some weird dream?"

"Read, great warrior. Prepare for battle by learning what the Father does for those who obey. Go to the book of Judges, chapters six and seven."

Ryan felt a heavy object hit his legs. He turned over in the dark room and sat up, wondering at the dream. The clock on the nightstand read *6:19.* He flipped on the bedside lamp and, squinting against the brightness, looked at what lay against his legs. *An open book?* He pulled it closer. The top of the page read Judges 6. His breath caught in his throat, and his heart rate increased.

He looked around the room. No one was there. The door was shut, and everything seemed to be exactly where he'd left it last night. He quietly got out of bed, opened the door, and peered out. *No one's up yet. Now what?*

He looked back at the Bible still lying on the bed. *Is it possible?* He walked over and sat down, picking it up.

The Israelites did evil in the eyes of the LORD, and for seven years he gave them into the hands of the Midianites. Because the power of Midian was so oppressive, the Israelites prepared shelters for themselves in mountain clefts, caves and strongholds.

Ryan read on, curious. Then he realized he was reading some of the same words Matthew had spoken to him. He paused to think back to the conversation and then looked again at the words the Lord spoke to Gideon. He grabbed a pen and began to underline the similarities and then read them over again.

"Verse 12, 'The Lord is with you, mighty warrior.' Verse 14, 'Go in the strength you have and save Israel out of Midian's hand. Am I not sending you?' And verse 23, 'But the LORD said to him, "Peace! Do not be afraid."' Did I just experience what I think I experienced?"

Ryan read on. As Israel walked away with a great victory, Ryan shook his head. *Now what? I don't see me leading anyone to defeat a great army. I don't understand. Maybe I am losing my mind.*

A gentle knock on his door caught his attention. He looked at the clock for the third time that morning. *Or is it only twice? 7:02.* He walked over and opened the door to see his mom standing there in her robe.

"I saw your light on." She smiled up at him. "Would you like some coffee?"

"Yeah, Mom. I think that would be a good idea."

Ryan waited in a room near the church altar, watching his parents walk slowly forward to the piano music through a crack in the door. He couldn't remember ever seeing his mom dressed up. The gold tea-length dress with empire ruched waist and lace bolero jacket complemented her, and he watched with admiration through the open door.

Next came Frank and Faye. Faye's plum-colored tea-length dress was a nice contrast to Victoria's gold, but the beaded trim added a touch of flamboyance that wouldn't have suited his mother.

The piano music changed, and Ryan looked over his shoulder at Peter. "Ready?"

Peter simply replied "Yes," his focus intent. *He's definitely ready,* thought Ryan.

Peter stepped out of the room first, followed by Logan, Andy, and Ryan. The four men in their tuxes lined the front steps, turning to watch Heather send Emma and Taylor down the aisle. Emma's navy blue satin dress rustled as she confidently walked down the aisle, but Taylor panicked, wrapping her arms around her crouching mother's neck. Heather returned her little girl's hug.

Logan stepped forward from the front of the church and crouched down as Heather pointed Taylor's gaze to her daddy. Cautiously at first, then running at her top speed, she charged down the aisle, past her sister and into Logan's arms as the congregation tittered. He scooped her up and whispered into her ear before handing her off to Faye and stepping back into his place.

As Heather stepped back into line, Ryan caught his first look at Brittney. Wow, he thought. The bodice of her strapless, navy blue chiffon dress fit snugly while the skirt flowed gracefully from a twist empire waist. Gentle dark curls were pulled back on one side with a simple pearl clip. *Beautiful.* Her eyes met his as she walked down the aisle, and Ryan didn't want to look anywhere else. He almost forgot to breathe.

First Allie and then Heather followed Brittney down the aisle, lining up in their assigned places. Then Amber stepped into full view of the congregation. The pianist started *The Bridal March,* and everyone stood. Amber's white dress, similar in style to her bridesmaids, included three simple beaded flowers at her waist and a chapel train. A simple halo of flowers rested on her head of long curls underneath the lace veil that hung to her waist. She loosely held a small bouquet of white roses, and while all eyes were on her, her eyes were solidly on Peter.

Before they knew it, the happy couple had exchanged vows, and the pastor introduced Mr. and Mrs. Peter Yager. The happy newlyweds led the way down the aisle, followed by Logan and Heather, Andy and Allie, and Ryan and Brittney. Ryan stood tall with Brittney on his arm, proudly escorting her to a small room just off the foyer.

The girls encircled the bride, chattering all at once while they worked to fasten her train up. Logan shook Peter's hand. "Congratulations, Pete. I'm proud of you."

"Thanks, Logan. I owe you quite a lot."

"Yeah, I know." He grinned at his brother.

"So, I'm guessing we're not running in the mornings for a while," said Andy.

Peter laughed. "Yeah, give me about a week, huh?"

"How long are you going to hang around the party?" asked Brittney.

Peter looked at Amber. "Do we have to go?"

She looked directly at him, smiling. "Nope."

He walked over and drew her into his arms. "Don't tempt me."

"Cut the cake and get out," suggested Heather. "No one's going to mind."

Faye knocked on the door and stuck her head in the room. "Everyone's outside."

"Okay, let's get out there," said Heather.

The bridesmaids and groomsmen all joined the group of people excitedly waiting outside in the chilly, late January afternoon. At last, Peter and Amber appeared at the top of the steps. Everyone cheered and threw rose petals as the couple made their way to Peter's Jeep.

Frank and Faye's home overflowed with people celebrating the wedding. Ryan headed out to the deck, pleased to see Brittney standing at the railing.

"The coat doesn't quite match the dress."

She glanced down at her light blue parka. "Colors clash?" She smiled up at him.

The mischievous smile that includes a twinkle in her eye. Her smiles were becoming irresistible to Ryan. "Yeah. Something like that."

She turned to lean against the railing. "You've lost your tie and cummerbund."

He stepped back and held his hands out to his side. "They weren't all that comfortable, but give me some credit. I stayed in the coat, pants, and dress shoes."

She laughed. "Too many people inside for you?"

He gave her half a nod. "A few. But your mom seems in her element."

"Yeah, she loves a party. Did Peter and Amber leave?"

"I think they snuck out about an hour ago."

"Good for them."

"Any chance of the rest of us skipping out on the party early?"

She laughed. "You, maybe. I've got to fight through that crowd to get to my room!"

"Have you heard any more on Grace?"

She looked down, stuffing her hands in the coat's pockets. "Melissa called early this morning before she left the hospital. Her oxygen saturation is continuing to drop."

Ryan knew enough to know the oxygen deprivation was going to bring her organs to a critical moment. Either things turned around soon, or the child's body would give up. "I'm sorry, B."

She looked at him, a tear escaping. "Gracie calls me that."

He reached out and gently wiped the tear with his thumb. The simple contact heightened his senses, and he looked her in the eye.

"Ryan! Brittney!" Faye threw open the dining room door and motioned to them, her face revealing panic. "We need you! Joshua just collapsed."

Ryan rushed inside to find Chad lifting Josh onto the couch. "What happened?"

"He just fell down," said Chad with anxiety in his eyes.

Ryan looked at the boy's chest and saw he was breathing. He

did a quick check over all his limbs and didn't notice any broken bones. "Did you get him to his doctor last week?"

"Yes," said his mother, Amy, as she hugged her husband's arm. "He said to just keep a watch on him. The nosebleeds were prob'ly nothing to worry about, he said."

Joshua started to stir a bit.

"What has he eaten today?" asked Brittney.

"Not much," said Amy helplessly. "He said his stomach was a-hurtin' him, and he didn't feel like eating."

Ryan locked eyes with Brittney. He looked back at Josh and saw he was awake.

"Hey, there, Josh," said Ryan, bending close. "Remember me?"

"Yeah."

"How are you feeling?"

"My head hurts."

He gently began feeling around the boy's head and neck. "Anything else?"

"My tummy hurts, too."

He gently felt the boy's stomach.

"What do you feel?" said Brittney.

"Something on the left side is swollen," said Ryan to Brittney.

"What's that mean?" said Frank.

"Check for bruising," said Brittney without answering her father.

Ryan pulled the boy's shirt up and looked around his abdomen. "Nothing obvious there." He pulled up his sweater sleeves and saw several small bruises in various stages of healing. "How long have these been here?"

"I don't exactly know," said Amy. She spread her hands out. "He's always showin' up with a new bruise. Seems like he can just about walk by something and get bruises from it."

Ryan clenched his jaw and looked at Brittney again. "You want to change clothes?"

"Give me three minutes."

"What's going on, son?" said Thomas.

He looked at Josh. "Why don't you lay right here for a minute while I talk to your mom and dad, okay?"

The little boy nodded, and Faye moved in to sit with him.

Ryan stood and looked at Chad and Amy. "Why don't we step over here?" The crowd parted, allowing them to get to the kitchen. Frank, Thomas, Logan, and Andy followed.

"Chad, I've already told you I'm not a doctor, and I certainly don't have any equipment here to help tell us what's going on."

"But you're worryin' about something," said Chad fearfully.

"Your son's symptoms lead me to believe that this is something critical," said Ryan. "I recommend we get him to a doctor immediately."

Amy grabbed Chad's hand. "But the clinic is closed on Saturdays."

Andy looked at Ryan. "You're recommending an ER in Portland?"

Ryan returned Andy's gaze, not sure how much he knew about the hospitals in Portland. *If I tell them I recommend going straight to Doernbecher, will anyone besides Brittney understand I'm concerned about cancer?*

"Son?" said Thomas as the silence lengthened.

Ryan sighed. "I recommend we take him straight to Doernbecher Children's Hospital," said Ryan. He watched the eyes of those in the small group around him. He saw realization in the eyes of Frank and Logan.

"I'm ready," said Brittney, hurrying back into the room in jeans and an Oregon Health and Science University sweatshirt.

"Chad, you and Amy go with Ryan and Brittney," said Logan. "We'll watch over Caleb. Take as long as you need."

Chapter 12

EVERYONE LOADED INTO BRITTNEY'S CAR, and Ryan got behind the wheel. She tried to remain objective as Ryan drove to Portland with Joshua and his parents in the back seat. She considered other medical possibilities that explained Joshua's symptoms, but cancer seemed the most likely. *Maybe it's just because you work in the oncology unit, she tried to convince herself.*

Ryan led the way into the ER unit, carrying Joshua. Thankfully, the place was unusually quiet for a Saturday afternoon. He went to the triage station and reported in as Chad and Amy hurried behind him, still wearing their Sunday best from attending the wedding earlier.

The nurse looked at Ryan, who was still in his tux pants and dress shirt. "Looks like something fancy got interrupted. What seems to be the problem today?"

Ryan spoke up. "Four–year-old patient presenting with long-term fatigue and multiple nosebleeds since suspected case of the flu in November. Parents report that he bruises easily and often. Patient passed out for approximately three to five minutes. Upon coming to, he complained of a stomachache and headache. He has a swollen spot on the left side of his abdomen and has eaten very little today."

The nurse raised her eyebrows at Ryan. "Medical field?"

"Paramedic out of McWilliam."

"Okay. Are the parents here?"

"Yes," said Chad, stepping forward.

"Your son's name?"

"Joshua."

The nurse looked appraisingly at the little boy. "Okay, Joshua. Why don't you come sit here for me? I'm just going to ask your parents a few more questions and get your vitals, okay?"

Joshua nodded as he sat down in the chair. The nurse got the basic information from Chad and Amy, and then she put a bracelet on Joshua.

"Do I have to stay here?" said Joshua, a nervous expression in his young eyes.

"The doctor will tell you that," said the nurse gently, "but first he has to know you're not feeling well." She pointed to the medical bracelet she'd just put on him. "This tells the doc that you need some attention, okay?"

Joshua nodded but leaned into his mother timidly. "Does my mom get to go with me?"

"Of course," said the nurse. "And your dad. The doctor will need their help too."

"Okay," said Joshua, holding tightly to Amy's hand.

"You all come with me," said the nurse. "Paramedic, you'll have to wait out here. Family only in the back."

Chad turned to look at Ryan uncertainly.

"You go ahead," said Ryan. "I'll wait for you."

"Here's my cell phone number," said Brittney, holding out a slip of paper that Chad took from her. "We'll be here in the hospital waiting for an update."

"Thanks," said Chad gratefully. His wife's wide-eyed glance met Ryan's eyes before she turned away.

Brittney and Ryan watched them walk through the doors. "What are you thinking?" said Brittney in a low voice.

"Nothing good," said Ryan, shaking his head.

"Same here."

"Well, it will probably be a while. Want to head over and check on Grace?"

Brittney looked at him in surprise. "Yeah, actually I would like that."

She led the way to the skybridge and then to the oncology ward. They walked into the locker room, and she grabbed two sets of isolation scrubs. After putting them on, they walked out to the nurse's station.

"Hey, there," she greeted the nurses on duty.

"Hey, Britt," said Melissa. "What are you doing here?"

"Brought friends to the ER and thought I'd stop in up here while we wait."

"Who's this friend?" said Jennifer, raising her eyebrows and looking over Ryan.

"My new sister-in-law's brother," said Brittney.

"Oh, that I should be cursed with a brother-in-law like you!" said Jennifer with a wink.

Ryan grinned.

"Stop it," said Brittney, laughing.

"Did the ER visit interrupt the wedding?" said Melissa, returning everyone to seriousness.

"No, thankfully," said Brittney. "Just the reception—and the bride and groom had already left."

Melissa pointed at Jennifer. "Before she completely loses her mind, Grace has been asking about you. Diane said she had a pretty good day. She's not shown any improvement, but her numbers are holding steady."

"Good. Thanks," said Brittney. She looked at Ryan. "Her room is this way."

They walked down the hall to Grace's room and paused outside her window. Brittney grabbed two masks. Handing one to Ryan, she said, "You don't have to come in here."

"I know that."

She returned his steady gaze for a moment, wondering if the charm she'd seen the past week was normal. *A girl could get used to this,* she thought. "Thanks."

He nodded. "Come on. Your girl's waiting on you."

He opened the door, and Brittney walked through. "Hey, Gracie!"

"B!" Gracie's voice was weak, but her smile lit up the room for Brittney. "Are you back?"

"No, sweetheart. Just visiting."

"I'm glad," said Grace. "I missed you. Who's he?"

"I'm Ryan." He came to stand beside the bed just behind Brittney.

"He's a friend of mine," said Brittney. "How do you like his outfit?"

"Looks fancy under the gown. Was the wedding today?" Grace asked.

"Yes," said Brittney.

"Were you beautiful?" said Grace.

"The most beautiful woman there," said Ryan.

Brittney looked at him. "You're supposed to say the bride was the most beautiful."

Ryan wrinkled his nose and looked at Grace. "The bride's my sister."

Grace giggled.

Brittney rolled her eyes at him and turned back to Grace. "The bride was very beautiful too."

"Did you get me a picture?" said Grace.

"I had one taken just for you," said Brittney. "I should have it for you when I come back to work on Tuesday."

Brittney glanced at the monitors. *O2 is down to 83.* "How are you feeling, Gracie?"

"Okay. Sometimes breathing gets hard."

"If you tell the nurses, they can give you some medicine to help," Brittney reminded her.

"It makes me sleepy," said Grace. "I don't want to sleep yet."

"What would you like, Grace?" said Ryan suddenly.

"Anything?" said Grace.

"Ryan," said Brittney quietly, wondering what kind of promise he might make.

"You tell me what it is, and we'll see what I can do," said Ryan.

"I'd really like a chocolate shake," said Grace, her small voice filled with hope. "It's been so long since I've been here, and what they bring is okay, but it's not like a real shake."

"Nurse B, what do you think?" said Ryan.

Brittney looked at Gracie. *She's so pale, Father.* "I think we could probably sneak in one chocolate milkshake."

"Yes!" said Ryan and Grace together.

"But," said Brittney, "you keep obeying the nurses."

"I will," said Grace.

"Okay," said Brittney. "We'll let you rest for a while."

"I'll be back tomorrow with that chocolate shake." Ryan winked at her and was rewarded with a smile.

They walked down the hall into the locker room. Brittney just got the door closed before the first tear fell.

"B?" said Ryan.

She couldn't answer. She covered her face with her hands, trying to control the tears that wanted to fall. She felt Ryan's hand on her shoulder.

"Brittney?"

His gentle concern was more than she could handle. She turned into his shoulder and let go. As the sobs began, she felt his arms encircle her.

Ryan picked up her phone and answered the vibration. "Brittney's phone... Yes... We'll be down in just a few minutes."

He closed the phone and turned toward Brittney. "Better?"

She turned from the sink, drying her face with a rough towel, and looked at him. "How bad do I look?"

"You look beautiful."

"Yeah, right. Either you're lying, or you're somehow biased."

Ryan put up his hands. "I plead the fifth."

"Chicken." Brittney tossed the towel into the laundry bin. "Was that Chad?"

"Yeah, they need our help."

Brittney and Ryan made their way back to the ER and found Chad and Amy in a triage room. Amy's eyes were as red as Brittney imagined her own were.

"Hey," said Brittney, sitting beside Amy. "What did the doctor say?"

"We're not sure of all the medical words," said Chad, "but he wants to do something called a marrow opsy. Do you know what that is?"

Brittney's heart sank.

"What else did he say?" said Ryan.

"He was talkin' about some A-L-L leukemia being what might be wrong," said Chad. He glanced at his wife before looking back at Ryan. "Leukemia kills people, don't it?"

"It can, but that depends on a lot of things," said Ryan.

"We'll know more after the bone marrow biopsy," said Brittney, "but acute leukemia isn't all bad. Leukemia accounts for about one-third of all childhood cancers, and most kids with ALL go into remission and live full lives."

"He said something about the blood tests showin' lots of white blood cells," said Amy anxiously.

"That's why's he's ordering the bone marrow test," said Brittney. "That will tell him for sure what kind of cancer we're looking at. "

"So we should do it?" said Chad.

"It's not going to be fun for Joshua," said Brittney, "but, yes. You should let them do the test."

Chapter 13

BRITTNEY WANTED TO STEP OUTSIDE to call her parents and update them on the situation, so Ryan walked her out and then sat on a bench nearby, alone with his thoughts. *What a couple of weeks! Joshua, Gracie, Brittney. Then there's the mob back at the Yager home.* Ryan rubbed his face. *I thought the wedding was going to be the stress point of my time here.*

Feeling restless, he stood up and paced a few steps to the stone face of the hospital building and leaned against it. *Chad and Amy are beginning to depend on me, but Brittney's better at the cancer stuff than I am. The wedding's over; I need to get back to McWilliam, anyway. Or decide if I'm going to try out Portland.*

He turned around to watch Brittney. Flashes of her passed through his mind as he thought of their discussion on the porch swing and in the kitchen, how beautiful she looked this morning and how fragile she'd been just a short time ago after seeing Gracie. He sighed deeply.

You were made for more than you've taken hold of.

Matthew! Is this why I'm being sent?

Silence.

Okay, God. If I buy into all this, You're the One sending me. Am I supposed to stick around and help Brittney through all this?

Silence.

He sighed again. "You know, I'm actually trying to get this."

You were made for more than you've taken hold of.

He looked at the sky. "Yeah. I'm sure that's supposed to be helpful, but I'm just not sure what to do with it."

"Are you talking to me?" said Brittney, clicking her phone closed and walking closer.

Ryan's head swiveled toward her voice. "Huh? Oh, no. Sorry. Everyone okay back in Crossing?"

"Yeah. The party broke up right after we left, so everyone pitched in to get things cleaned up. Logan and Heather have gone home, and your mom and dad were just hanging around to see if we needed anything else. My mom's going to make a pallet for Caleb in her room and put him to bed shortly."

"Sounds like things are under control."

"I am so tired," said Brittney. "It's been such a long day."

"You have no idea," said Ryan, more to himself than to her.

"What do you mean?" Brittney prodded.

Unwilling to share his thoughts, Ryan turned to humor. "I'm still in a tux."

She smiled back. "It could be the latest thing in paramedic wear," she teased. Then she gazed at him steadily. "Come on. Quit deflecting."

"Ouch. Well, the truth is I'm not sure you'd believe me if I told you. I'm not sure I believe it." Ryan put his hands in his pockets and looked away. "You ever feel like you've been given a message from God, but you're not sure what to do with it?"

"Sure. Sometimes it feels like I do more wondering what to do with it than knowing where to go next. You thinking about your career options again?"

Ryan met her gaze. "I suppose. Two weeks ago, McWilliam didn't seem like it was that far away. Now, well... I just don't know."

"Is your family growing on you?"

He looked at her for a moment, considering the question. "Maybe. And maybe a few others too."

She brushed her hair behind her ear. He was beginning to recognize that motion as discomfort.

"Before I got here, I dreaded coming. I didn't know what to expect out of Rach-, er, Amber, much less the family she was marrying into. And my dad and I haven't always gotten along."

"In what way?"

"I feel like I've disappointed him, that being a paramedic wasn't what he wanted for me. I think he wanted me by his side looking for Rach." Ryan shook his head. "I've got to get used to calling her Amber."

Brittney put her hands in her jacket pocket and shrugged. "It's okay. I'm sure it's a tough change."

"Anyway, things are different from what I thought they'd be."

"In a good way?"

She looked at him. He decided he could get lost in those eyes. "Yeah, very good."

"Want to go down to the cafeteria and get some coffee?"

"Sure. Lead the way."

⁂

Ryan rolled over and looked at the clock. *9:17.* By the time the hospital got Amy and Joshua settled into a room, it had been almost one o'clock in the morning. He'd driven Chad and Brittney back, watching Brittney let herself in her parent's front door before he and Chad walked down the road just a bit to get their cars. After that, he had gone home and barely removed the tuxedo before falling into bed.

He grabbed clothes and jumped in the shower, hoping the hot water would help his foggy brain recover. Ten minutes later, he walked into the kitchen to find his mom pouring a cup of fresh coffee and his dad reading the paper.

"I heard you in the shower, so I started a fresh pot."

"Thanks, Mom."

"How were Chad and Amy when you left last night?" said Victoria.

"Still pretty shaken," said Ryan, taking a sip of the coffee.

"Did you find out any more?" said Thomas.

"No. They weren't expecting the results from the bone marrow test until they talked to a doctor this morning."

"Did you suspect cancer yesterday, son?" said Thomas.

"Yeah, Dad. I did."

"Was that kind of thing you were doing over the holidays?" said Victoria.

Ryan wondered if his parents would ever put Christmas to

rest. *It was past, done. Can we move on?* Aloud, he said, "Kinda." He took a sip of his coffee. "I had to take three anatomy and physiology classes and some first aid and trauma care type classes for my license, but I've picked up a lot during clinicals and hanging around the ERs."

"You know, the clinic is looking to hire someone full time," said Victoria in the tone moms get when they have an idea that they want their children to act on.

"I'm not a doctor, Mom," said Ryan, knowing where this conversation was leading.

"I know," said Victoria. "But sometimes they have trouble getting a doctor down here regularly. And lots of folks complain because the only person who's always there is the receptionist. Even the nurses rotate down from Portland. It'd be nice to have someone there with medical knowledge who knows more about you than just what you want to be seen for on one particular visit."

"I'd bet you could probably handle a lot of what happens in Crossing," said Thomas, joining forces with his wife. "Seasonal type things like colds and flus, sprained muscles, and that type of thing."

"You can't sprain a muscle, Dad," said Ryan.

"Just something for you to think about," said Thomas innocently.

Ryan paused to look at his dad. *Just something to think about. No debate? No pushing the issue farther?*

"Well, we better get moving if we're going to make it to church," said Victoria. "Did Keith ever come back upstairs?"

"I haven't seen him, dear," said Thomas.

"He's probably organizing some tool or supply down in the store," said Victoria.

"I'll get him, Mom, and meet you over at church," said Ryan.

He grabbed his jacket and headed downstairs. "Keith? You down here?"

"Right here. Just straightening up these paintbrushes."

"Want to walk over to church with me?"

"Sure. I'll get my coat."

The two boys headed out the door and down the sidewalk two blocks to the church building. The day was unseasonably warm for the last few days of January in Oregon, and the sun shone brightly on Ryan's back.

"So, do you think you and Brittney will be the next to get married?" asked Keith casually.

The question snapped Ryan out of his thoughts. "What? Why would you ask a crazy question like that?"

Keith shrugged. "Just wondering. You look at her different from the way you look at all the other women."

"I do, huh?" Ryan considered this for a minute. *She is nice to look at.*

"You're smiling," said Keith.

"You're annoying this morning." Ryan reached over and messed up Keith's hair.

Keith laughed as he pulled away. He moved back to walk beside Ryan, straightening his hair. "If you do, does that mean you'll move to Portland?"

Ryan shook his head ruefully. "Not that I'm admitting to anything, but would you like that?"

"It's closer than McWilliam."

"True."

"I'd rather have you here with us."

Ryan sighed and ran a hand through his hair. "I don't know what's going to happen. But you'll be one of the first to know when I figure it out."

Sitting behind Brittney during church proved distracting. Ryan had to keep refocusing on the service, and he kept glancing over at Keith to see the boy smiling at him like he knew exactly what Ryan was thinking. *The boy's too smug for sixteen!*

The service ended, and Ryan stood as Brittney turned to pick up her purse and Bible. *Dark circles are beginning to form under her eyes.* "How'd you sleep?"

"Okay," said Brittney.

"Liar," said Ryan, smiling to soften the effect.

"Yeah, well. I'm a liar. You're a chicken." Her eyes twinkled in response, almost like she was daring him to challenge her.

"When are you heading home?" said Ryan, redirecting the conversation back to safer ground.

"Later this afternoon. I have to be back at work on Tuesday, and I'd like to get some things done at home first. What are you going to do?"

"I think I'll check out a couple places in Portland before heading back to McWilliam."

"Excuse me." Ryan's mom couldn't have missed what Ryan had just said. Ryan and Brittney both looked at her. "Do you have plans this afternoon, Ryan?"

"At some point I need to head into Portland, Mom, but the time doesn't matter too much. Why?"

"Well, Faye and I were just talking," said Victoria, gesturing toward where Faye stood. "Brittney, why don't you and your parents join us for lunch? It's nothing fancy, but I'd be pleased if you'd come."

Ryan looked at his mom suspiciously for a moment. *Is she pushing us together?*

"Your Dad and I are going to run home first," Faye told Brittney. "I want to change clothes and grab some of the leftovers from the wedding."

"Sounds good," said Brittney. "I'll ride along and change too."

"Yes!" said Keith with a fist pump.

Ryan elbowed him in the chest, sending him flying back onto the pew.

"Ow!" said Keith. He broke out in giggles as he stood back up and rubbed his chest.

"Ryan!" Victoria scolded.

"Don't ask, Mom," said Ryan.

Brittney looked from Keith to Ryan, smiling as she turned to follow Faye out the door.

Chapter 14

BRITTNEY THREW ON HER WHITE cashmere sweater and a comfy pair of jeans before packing her skirt into the suitcase. Taking one final look around the room, she zipped it up and carried it downstairs. Faye walked out from her bedroom just as Brittney reached the bottom step.

"Do you have everything, dear?"

"I think so, Mom. If not, I'll be back for Amber's birthday celebration in three weeks."

"Are you two ready to go?" said Frank as he walked out of the bedroom behind his wife.

"Let's hit the road," said Brittney.

Brittney followed her parents back to town in her own purple Chevy Equinox so she could leave for home after she ate. Her thoughts kept turning to Ryan. *Does he want more than just friendship from me? Father, he's not proved himself trustworthy in the long-term category from what he says about job-hopping every few months. So what do I do if he does move to Portland? It would be nice to hang around him. Do I set a time limit? Find out the longest he's been at previous jobs? Ugh! Father, it would be great if you'd speak up here. Of course, I probably have to shut up long enough to let you speak, huh?*

Brittney sighed. *It would be so easy to talk myself into taking a risk with him. Father, help me be wise. To follow You, not necessarily my heart.*

She parked beside her dad's truck in front of Micah's Hardware. Keith let them in the front door. Walking upstairs, Brittney was greeted by a smorgasbord of cold cuts, cheeses, bags of chips, crescent rolls, and Ryan dressed casually in faded blue jeans and a light blue sweater that matched his eyes. She almost missed the top step.

He reached out to help her. "You okay?"

She smiled up at him, her hand tingling in his warm clasp. "Yeah."

"Why do I think we're back to that lying chicken?"

"What's a lying chicken?" said Thomas, glancing away from the TV.

Ryan grinned at Brittney. "Nothing, Dad."

Everyone grabbed plates and began to dive into the meats when Brittney's cell phone rang. She popped a piece of cheese into her mouth and went to check the number. When she saw the screen, she immediately answered the call and started down the stairs.

"Hello."

"Hey, Britt. It's Diane."

"What's up?"

"Thought I'd give you a heads up. Her kidneys are failing."

Brittney closed her eyes. "Okay. Who's working tonight?"

"Nicole."

"Thanks, Diane."

"You're welcome. And Britt?"

"Yeah?"

"I'm sorry."

"Yeah." Brittney hung up the phone and stood at the bottom of the stairs trying to gather herself.

"Is it Grace?" said Ryan.

She turned and saw him standing just five steps up. "Yes. Her kidneys are failing."

Ryan breathed in deeply. "Are you heading out now?"

"Yeah. I've got to get to the hospital."

"Let me tell everyone what's going on and grab my coat."

"Ryan…"

"I'll follow you up there. Besides, I owe her a shake."

Brittney smiled. "Yeah, you do. Okay."

Ryan ran up the stairs. She could hear him explaining to their parents about Gracie making a turn for the worse and that they were going to see her. It wasn't long before he was back down the stairs with her jacket and purse.

"You might want these."

"Thanks." She plucked her keys out of her coat pocket and led the way out the door.

"I'll follow you into town, then find a place to get the shake once we get close. I'll meet you at her room."

Brittney nodded as she swung into the driver's seat and started the engine. *Hang on Gracie. I'm coming.*

Brittney steeled herself as she walked into the room. As usual, there were no parents in sight. "Hey, Gracie."

Weak from fighting the lymphoma, she barely turned her head on the pillow. "Hey, B. Where's Ryan?"

"He stopped to get a chocolate milkshake."

"He remembered?"

"Of course he did." Brittney glanced at the nearly empty urine bag and picked up the chart. *Less than 70mL all day.* The monitors showed her O2 stats down to 75 and the EKG pulsed with longer, more erratic intervals.

"I brought you a picture," said Brittney. She held up a three by five photo.

Grace's face lit up. "You are beautiful! No wonder he likes to look at you."

"Who?"

"Ryan."

"What are you talking about?"

"When he was here yesterday, he looked at you a whole lot more than he looked at me."

"Really?" Brittney couldn't believe she was having this conversation with Grace. "How about we change the subject? How about you tell me what you saw today?"

"A new boy came in sometime last night. I think maybe he's the same age as me."

"When did you see him?"

"They took him for some tests this morning just after breakfast."

"Can I come in?" said Ryan from the door. He peered with

great exaggeration up and down the hall behind him, then in a stage whisper, he said, "I have contraband."

Grace smiled at him. "What's contraband?"

Brittney leaned in close. "It's something you're not supposed to have."

Grace's eyes lit up. "Is it chocolate?"

"Well, I wouldn't swear to it," said Ryan, bringing it from behind his back, "but it does have a suspicious brown color. And I believe I saw the very expert milkshake maker put an extra helping of chocolate syrup into it. Are you up to eating some?"

"Yeah."

Brittney adjusted Grace's bed up a little while Ryan opened the plastic spoon and pulled the lid off the cup. He dipped the spoon into the ice cream and offered Grace a small bite.

"Oh, yum. That's really good."

Brittney watched amazed at how well Ryan interacted with Gracie. Saving her from the embarrassment of admitting how weak she was, he patiently fed the little girl as much as she wanted. He had her laughing about a ridiculously dressed woman at the ice cream shop and a man in the lobby with a big nose. Before Brittney knew it, shift change was over, and Nicole was knocking on the door.

"How are things going in here?" said Nicole.

"Hi, Nicole," said Grace.

"Hey, sweet girl. How are you feeling?"

"I'm a little tired."

"Do you want your bed down a little?" said Nicole.

"No," said Grace. "Not yet."

Nicole got busy checking lines, wires and vitals, making notations on the chart, and watching the monitors. After a few minutes, she looked at Brittney. She didn't need Nicole's confirmation that Gracie was probably down to her last hours.

"I'll be at the desk if you need anything, sweetheart," said Nicole to Grace. Before walking out of the room, she closed the blinds on the hall window most of the way. "Just to give you some privacy," she said to Brittney. "Call if you need anything." Brittney nodded and watched Nicole walk out the door.

"You know what I miss?" said Grace.

"What?" said Ryan.

"I miss cuddling with my mom while we watch TV."

Brittney swallowed hard as she walked closer to Gracie. Such a simple thing, cuddling. The loving touch of another person that most people took for granted.

"My mom's not brave like you, B," said Grace. "She scares easy."

I've been right all along about this young mother, thought Brittney. *She's scared and weak, and instead of encouraging her, instead of loaning her some of my strength, I judged her. Father, forgive me!*

"Don't be sad, B," said Grace. "You're going to be okay." She looked at Ryan. "You found someone who's strong like you."

Brittney looked at Ryan, the tears barely kept under control. He searched her eyes, asking unspoken questions, then reached out for her gloved hand. Brittney squeezed hard, relying for the moment on his strength.

Brittney came to a decision. "I'll be right back, Gracie."

Brittney walked out to the nurse's station, pulled off her

gloves, and dialed the number for Grace's mom at the Ronald McDonald House. "Hi, this is Brittney Yager, one of your daughter's nurses."

"Yes?" said the young mother fearfully on the other end of the phone line.

"Ma'am, your daughter's kidneys are failing."

"I... I know."

Brittney struggled to maintain her professionalism. "She may not live through the night."

The quiet on the other end of the phone was only broken by small sniffles and the background noise of other residents at the Ronald McDonald house.

Brittney continued to reach out to her. "Wouldn't you like to come sit with her for a bit?" Brittney paused, waiting.

"Okay," said the mother at last. "I'll be right over."

When Grace's mother arrived, Brittney helped her into the isolation garments. They walked into the room and found Ryan sitting close to Grace's head, watching cartoons with her. Grace barely turned her head to see who had entered her room.

"Mommy," she said weakly. "You came back."

"Why don't I help you crawl into bed beside her?" said Brittney softly, guiding the hesitant woman forward and willing her voice not to crack.

The mother looked at Brittney gratefully with tears in her eyes. She nodded. "Thank you," she whispered.

As Brittney carefully held lines and wires, Grace's mother crawled into the bed and reached out for her daughter. "Come here, baby."

Brittney gently covered the two up with a blanket and then faded into the background with Ryan.

Chapter 15

RYAN GRATEFULLY SIPPED THE COFFEE Nicole brought him. Standing outside Grace's room, he watched as Brittney said her final goodbyes. The sweet child died at 11:43pm, content in her mother's arms.

Brittney walked out, rubbing her eyes.

"Want some coffee?" asked Ryan.

"No," said Brittney in a low, tremulous voice. "I just want to go home."

"Come on. I'm driving you home. No argument. I'll come up again tomorrow and bring you back here to get your car. I want to stop in and see Josh anyway."

Brittney just nodded.

Ryan put his arm around her and guided her to the locker room where they shed their isolation gear. Then he led her down to the parking lot and put her in his Mustang.

At her condo, he walked her to the door. "Are you going to be okay tonight?"

She sighed. "Yeah."

"Call me in the morning when you wake up."

"You need sleep too."

"B, this is non-negotiable. Call me."

"Okay. Thank you… for everything."

"You're welcome. Good night."

Ryan watched her go in, then got back in his car and started for Crossing.

Well, at least that situation's resolved. Maybe not a great ending, but at least the stress of not knowing is over.

Ryan thought about Brittney's concern and care for Grace. *She's quite a woman. Smart, compassionate, quick-witted.*

Pictures of her came to Ryan's mind without effort: curled up on the porch swing, laughing during the card game, talking with him in the kitchen. Thoughts of settling down in one place had never been in Ryan's top priorities. *But Brittney is worth considering.* The thought almost surprised him. *Is this part of Your plan, God?*

Ryan mulled over this for a few minutes. "This sure would be easier, God, if You spoke to me like You spoke to Gideon."

You have not because you ask not.

The verse echoed through his mind. Ryan hesitated to ask God for much of anything. "You're not Santa Claus." *And I don't want to seem greedy.*

Ryan waivered until thoughts of his sister came to mind. *Rachel-Amber seems so relaxed with her relationship with You, God. She talks about You like she really is Your daughter. I guess that's a key difference. She's accepted the gift of being Your child. I'm still stuck on the fact that You are God.* Ryan sighed.

"Okay, my dad wants to be someone I go to for advice so I'm

guessing You do too. Can you please tell me what to do with my career? Should I stay in McWilliam? Or move to Portland? Or some third option I'm not considering right now? Like the clinic in Crossing. Is that a viable option?"

Ryan waited for a moment to see if something would happen. "Well, I guess even Gideon had to wait until morning for his answer."

✖✖✖✖✖✖✖✖✖

Ryan woke up in the morning to voices downstairs in the hardware store. He rolled over onto his back, rubbing his face. *Ugh. I feel awful.*

A knock sounded on his door. "Yeah?"

His Mom peeked in. "Ryan, honey. I'm sorry to wake you, but Daniel is downstairs with Eleni."

"Who?" Ryan opened one eye to look at his mom.

"Sorry, honey. Daniel is the cook over at the diner, and Eleni is his four–year-old daughter."

Ryan closed both eyes again. "Okay. Cook and daughter. Got it."

"Eleni's hurt, and there's no one at the clinic yet. Word's gotten out about what you did for Joshua the other day, and, well, he's wondering if you'll take a look."

Ryan groaned. "What time is it?"

"About 9:20."

"That late? What time does this clinic of yours open?"

"Usually 9:00, but sometimes the doctors don't make it down until later. Especially around weekends."

Ryan searched through his groggy brain to remember what day it was. "It's Monday, Mom."

"Yes." From the tone she used, it was clear she wondered what difference that made.

Is Monday really considered "near" a weekend rather than the start of the work week? He looked at her. Apparently so, since she's still look- ing at me. "All right. Tell them I'll be down in a minute."

"Thank you, honey." She closed the door.

"Mom!" said Ryan.

"Yes?" She opened the door just a crack.

"Can you get me some coffee, please? The stronger, the better."

"It'll be waiting on you."

"Thanks," muttered Ryan. He sat up in bed and ran his hands through his hair. What a way to start the day. He grabbed a pair of jeans and picked a clean t-shirt out of his suitcase, sliding it on as he walked down the hallway.

"You look like morning sunshine," said Thomas with a mis- chievous smirk.

Ryan looked at his dad and raised one eyebrow. "Thanks. Coffee?"

Thomas pointed to a cup on the counter. "How's the child?"

Ryan clenched his jaw. "She died about midnight."

Thomas grew solemn. "Sorry to hear that, son."

"Yeah. Me too." Ryan looked into his coffee for a moment and then took a couple of gulps before heading downstairs. He saw a man and child standing near the back of the store with his mom.

"Daniel, this is my son, Ryan."

Daniel shook Ryan's hand firmly. "Thank you for seeing us.

She fell this morning on an icy patch. As long as we don't touch her arm, she's fine, but she starts to cry whenever she has to use it."

"What's her name again?" said Ryan.

"Eleni," said Daniel.

Ryan crouched down to get eye level with the girl. "Hi, Eleni. How are you?"

"Your hair is sticking up," said Eleni with just a hint of disapproval in her voice.

"Yeah, well, you got me out of bed this morning," said Ryan as he ran a hand over his hair.

"You slept late," said Eleni.

"I was trying to. How about you tell me what hurts."

"Nothing."

"Hmmm." Ryan rubbed his unshaven chin. "What if you tell me what hurts if you move it."

"My arm."

"Can I take a look at it?"

Eleni looked at her father. "It's okay, beautiful one," said Daniel. "He will help you."

"Tell you what. You let me see your arm, and when I'm all done, if your dad says it's okay, we'll take a walk over to the general store and get a candy bar."

Eleni's eyes got big, and she looked at her dad again. He nodded at her, and she looked back at Ryan. "Okay."

Ryan looked at the girl's arm, feeling around the ulna and radius. "Does that hurt at all?"

She shook her head, but as he got closer to her elbow she began to cry. "Ow. Stop, please stop."

Ryan stopped touching but knew he needed to get a look at her elbow. "Eleni, I need to pull up your sweater so I can see your elbow, okay? Can you help me?"

With Daniel's help, they slowly pushed the sweater above Eleni's elbow. Ryan looked closely and didn't see anything wrong. He pushed a little on her arm closer to her shoulder. "Does it hurt up here at all?"

She shook her head.

Ryan took her hand in his and felt normal body temperatures in her fingers. "Now, that wasn't too bad, was it?"

She shook her head again.

"What is your favorite toy?" Ryan gently held onto the child's hand while he moved his other hand to her injured elbow.

"I like my building blocks!"

"Blocks, huh?" Without breaking eye contact, Ryan slowly pulled her arm down, straightening the arm with her palm facing up. "Do you have wood blocks, or are they different colors?"

"Oh, they are all kinds of different colors. But my favorite is the yell—"

Ryan quickly bent her elbow, pushing her hand up to her shoulder and hearing the faint pop of the bone moving back into place.

"You bent my—Daddy, he bent my arm." Eleni stood there bending and straightening her arm with a look of amazement. "It doesn't hurt."

Ryan grinned at her and stood.

Daniel beamed at him. "Thank you. Thank you."

"It was just a small dislocation. She should be fine now, but keep an eye on it. The ligaments may allow it to slip out of place again, so try to get her to go easy on it for a couple weeks to give them a chance to fully heal. A sling for a couple days would be okay if she tends to be rough on it."

"Yes, okay. Thank you so much," said Daniel.

Eleni spoke up. "Mr. Ryan. You said if I let you look at my arm, then I get candy."

Ryan chuckled. "Yes, I did. Will you give me just a minute to put on shoes?"

"If I give you two, will you comb your hair too?" said Eleni.

Chapter 16

BRITTNEY OPENED HER FRONT DOOR on the second knock.

"Pizza?" said Ryan.

"What kind?"

"Romano's pepperoni with a side of soda, chaperone included." Ryan moved to the side slightly and thumbed back towards his Mustang. Keith was trying to get a bag of two liters out of the back floorboard without dropping his backpack from his shoulder.

"Lucky guess on my favorite pizza?"

"Nope, smart detective work. I called your mom."

Brittney raised her eyebrows. *He called Mom?* "I'm impressed," she said.

"Hey, there," said Keith, finally walking up with the sodas.

"Hey, Keith. Come on in, guys," said Brittney. From the narrow entryway, she led the way around the corner to her kitchen, leaving Keith to close the door. She went to the cabinets to get plates and glasses. *Don't get excited or read anything into this,* she thought. *It's just pizza. My favorite kind. And he called Mom. I've got to stop arguing with myself.*

"Did you take it slow this morning?" said Ryan. He sat the pizza box and a short stack of napkins on the counter.

"As ordered," said Brittney, placing the plates and cups next to the pizza. "What time did I call you? About 10:00? After that I took a long shower and have just been flipping through channels on the television since then."

"Now it's my turn to be impressed," said Ryan. "You actually followed instructions."

Pointing at him, she said, "Don't count on it happening a lot. How about we pray before the pizza gets cold."

Keith volunteered to say a quick prayer, and then Ryan opened the box so everyone could grab a slice.

"Ryan was a hero again this morning," said Keith as he opened one of the sodas.

"He was?" said Brittney, surprised.

"You talk too much, Keith," said Ryan as he opened another soda and poured it into a glass.

"Eleni came in with a dislocated elbow," said Keith as he reached into the box for a steaming slice of pizza. "He calmed her down and before she knew it, he popped it right back into place! It was actually pretty amazing."

"Really," said Brittney, looking thoughtfully at Ryan. "Maybe you should open up an office in Crossing."

Ryan held his hands up in protest. "I'm not a doctor."

"Dad wants him to work at the clinic," Keith confided to Brittney.

Ryan in Crossing. The idea pleased her, which also disturbed her.

"Maybe you should," said Brittney as she poured herself a drink.

"What part of 'I'm not a doctor' is everyone missing?" said Ryan in exasperation.

"Being a paramedic is partway there," said Brittney. "Plus, you seem to have a natural ability for it, and you were great with both Joshua and…" Brittney's breath suddenly caught in her throat. She took a deep breath. She was not going to be able to continue if she looked at Ryan's sympathetic eyes right now, so she focused on her drink. "You've been great with all the kids I've seen you with. Why not finish your bachelor's and apply for med school?"

"I don't know," said Ryan, helping himself to a second slice of pizza. "What am I going to do for income while I'm in med school? That's quite a stretch, and not exactly something people do while working full time."

"True," said Brittney, moving out of the way so that Keith could get a second slice, "but you have a lot of practical experience already that will make some of it easier. When do you have to be back in McWilliam?"

"By the end of the week," said Ryan as he chewed.

"That stinks," said Keith around a mouthful of pizza.

"Yeah. Well, I'm back to work tomorrow," said Brittney, biting into her own slice.

"Are you sure that's a good idea?" said Ryan as he squelched a burp.

Brittney looked at him for a moment before dropping her gaze to her half-eaten pizza. "I don't have a choice. This isn't a situation where she was a close relative. I'll be pushing it asking for time off to go to the funeral."

"What if they don't let you go?" said Ryan.

"Diane's already said she'd cover for me. Worst case, I just switch shifts with her one day." She reached for a napkin.

Ryan nodded as he finished the last bite of his slice. After taking a drink, he said, "Whenever you're ready, we can go get your car. While we're there, I'm going to stop in and see Joshua."

"That sounds good. How about I go get my shoes while you two clean up." She tossed her crumpled napkin at Ryan. "Trash is under the sink."

"Hey!" said Keith, working on his third slice.

Brittney giggled and walked down the hallway.

✖✖✖✖✖✖✖✖✖

Ryan pulled up behind Brittney's car. She slid out of the front seat and peered back inside to thank him for the ride.

"We'll go find a parking space and meet you at the locker room." Ryan said.

Brittney nodded. "Sounds good. I just want to grab my phone, and I'll be right in."

She unlocked her car door, pulled her phone out of the center console, and checked for missed calls and voice mail. *Only missed Mom's call last night. Good.* She slid her phone into her purse and made her way into the hospital.

Well, God, what do I make of all his time at the hospital yesterday, not leaving when Gracie got bad? And what about the whole calling my mom to find out my favorite comfort food? I really need Your perspective on all this. I can't think clearly when he's around.

Just as Brittney made her way toward the elevators, Keith's backpack caught her eye. She turned to see Ryan and Keith standing in the entry talking to Stephanie. *The woman pursued Pete relentlessly, and now she's got Ryan cornered? Over my dead body!*

Brittney strode over to the trio and mischievously linked her arm into Ryan's. If he was surprised, he didn't give her any indication. "Hello, Stephanie."

Stephanie gave her a cool glance. "Brittney."

"You two know each other?" said Ryan.

"You could say that," said Brittney, choosing not to elaborate.

"Yes. I didn't realize you knew Ryan," said Stephanie.

"Oh, yes," said Brittney. "We've been spending a lot of time together lately." Brittney watched Stephanie's eyes narrow slightly. *Father, forgive me, but this blonde in her Armani pants and Jimmy Choo pumps can leave my family alone!*

"Well, isn't that fortunate for you," said Stephanie.

"Yes, it is," said Brittney brightly. "We just spent the weekend celebrating Peter's wedding."

"Hmmm. Yes. Well, I must be going," said Stephanie. She pulled a card from her purse and handed it to Ryan. "Perhaps we can meet another time," she said in a warmer tone than she had used with Brittney. She slipped a look at Brittney before walking off, leaving Brittney seething.

As they made their way to the elevators, Keith burst out, "Wow! She did not like you, Brittney!"

"What did I just walk away from?" asked a confused Ryan.

Brittney looked at Ryan and then Keith. "It's better if I keep my mouth shut. I have trouble finding anything nice to say about that woman." She held out her hand, palm up. "Where's that card?"

Ryan held up the card. Brittney grabbed it and quickly ripped it into small pieces in a fine display of temper.

Ryan raised an eyebrow. "Glad I wasn't going to call her."

"Don't even pretend," said Brittney hotly. "That snooty—"

"I thought you were going to keep your mouth shut?" said Ryan.

Brittney inhaled deeply, immediately ashamed of her behavior. "I was. Am. Ugh. Sorry."

"And I'm guessing all this has something to do with Peter?" said Ryan.

"Yeah, you could say that. She's just looking for a handsome man to hang on when she goes out about town."

"Handsome, huh?" said Ryan. He waggled an eyebrow at Brittney.

She looked at him and rolled her eyes. "Don't make me sorry for saving you!"

"I'm not sure 'saving' is the right word for what happened back there," said Ryan, grinning.

Brittney led the way into the locker room and showed Keith how to scrub and put on the isolation gown. Diane looked up as they arrived at the nurse's station.

"Brittney! What are you doing here?"

"The kid that came in Saturday night, Joshua," said Brittney. "He's a friend of the family. How much do you know about his case?"

"He's looking pretty good so far. Looks like it's ALL and caught pretty early."

"What's that mean?" said Keith.

"ALL is a type of leukemia," said Ryan.

"And it has an excellent remission rate," said Brittney. "His chances of survival are very high." Turning back to Diane, she said, "Can we see him?"

"Sure, just keep it short," said Diane. "I think both his parents are in there. End of the hall on the left."

They walked down the hall and knocked on Joshua's door. Chad answered, his face relaxing when he saw Ryan. "I'm so glad you came!" he said, reaching out to shake Ryan's hand. "Josh, look who's here!"

Brittney went over to hug Amy, while Ryan went straight to Josh's bed, leaving Keith standing uncertainly in the doorway. "Hey, little man. How are you feeling?"

"Okay," said Josh. "Did you know they have video games here? Can you play with me?"

"Well, to be honest, I'm not that good," said Ryan. "But, my brother Keith here is top notch."

Josh looked adoringly at Keith. "You are? Will you play with me?"

"Absolutely!" said Keith, coming to the bedside. "What do you want to play?"

As the two boys got busy on their controllers, Ryan drew Chad and Amy to the other side of the room to talk, and Brittney followed. "How are you doing?"

"Okay," said Chad. "Doc says he's pretty sure it's a kind of leukemia that they can fix."

"Yes," said Brittney. "He may get pretty sick during treatment, but they should be able to kill all the cancer cells, and then with some maintenance therapy, Josh can enjoy a long life."

Chad looked at Ryan. "Will you be 'round to help us with all that? I know he's in good hands here, but at home…."

Ryan gave a slight shake of his head. "I'm not sure how much I'll be around," said Ryan.

"It's just all new to us," said Amy, leaning against her husband, one hand gently rubbing her 16-week pregnant belly. "We're nervous, but I'm sure it'll all be fine by the time we go home."

"The nurses here are excellent," said Brittney, winking at Amy. "We won't let you go home until we're sure you know what to do."

"We just owe you so much for getting us here when you did," said Chad. "The doc said you had real good instincts."

Chapter 17

RYAN THOUGHT ABOUT THE EVENTS of the last couple weeks as he pulled into McWilliam. *God, are you really providing me the answer I asked for? Dad starts talking about the town clinic, Mom pipes in about how much they need someone consistent, and You bring me not only Joshua but also Eleni's dislocated elbow and Billy's sprained ankle. Moving is the right idea, I think, but maybe moving to Portland's the wrong idea? What about Brittney?*

Brittney circled through his thoughts the rest of the drive to the fire station. *Her old-fashioned accountability has me bringing Keith to go see her. Her family has me thinking about the future with all of them in my life, not just her. That impish smile of hers. The sparkle was missing from her eyes when I left the hospital. Probably just tired from the last week or so.*

Ryan sighed deeply. *When did my life get so complicated? About the same time Mom and Dad found Rachel. Amber. I've got to get used to calling her Amber,* he chastised himself again.

Lost in his thoughts, Ryan drove through town automatically. He turned left off the frontage road onto Williamette Drive, just two blocks from the fire department,

Crash.

Stunned momentarily from the jolt of the impact, Ryan shook his head before looking around him. One car sat to his left, crunched into his front fender. In the car, a young girl cried with her hands waving frantically up beside her head.

Ryan released his seatbelt, walked over to her driver's side window without a glance back at his beloved car, and knocked. "Are you okay?"

The young driver turned her blue eyes at him, big tears making their way down her cheeks. "I'm so sorry. My dad's gonna kill me. I'm sorry. I'm sorry." Her red ponytail wagged as she shook her head from side to side.

"Okay. Slow down and take a deep breath for me." Ryan looked at her friend in the passenger seat. Her hands were braced on the dashboard, and she stared straight out the windshield.

He looked quickly over both of them. No obvious broken bones or signs of bleeding through their sweatshirts and jeans.

"Dude!" A young man came running over from the sidewalk.

"Do you know these girls?" said Ryan hopefully.

"Yeah, from school."

"Know their home phone numbers? Or a parent's cell phone."

"Yeah."

"Call and ask them to get out here," said Ryan as he walked over to the passenger side. He'd just opened the car door when Sheriff Jeff Campbell pulled up behind the car. He nodded to the lanky sheriff before crouching down to talk to the passenger.

"Can you hear me?"

The girl turned her face toward him. She was very pale, and her brown eyes seemed to take up her whole face.

"Does anything hurt?" Ryan gently took her right hand from the dash and moved her hand up and down. Then he did the same with her left hand.

"That hurts some," she said quietly.

He looked her in the eye and smiled reassuringly. "Okay." He gently laid her hand in her lap. "Let's get that checked when the EMTs get here."

She nodded, nervously nibbling on her bottom lip.

"Just sit tight for the moment," said Ryan, standing up and looking for the sheriff.

The ambulance was just pulling up beside the sheriff's car, so Ryan walked over. His regular partner was stepping out of the passenger side. "Griffin! About time you got back to work!"

Ryan smiled and gave him the update on the girls. The second EMT listened closely and went to the car to check the passenger's wrist.

"You feel okay?"

"Yeah." Ryan moved his neck, gently stretching it out. "I'm fine."

Ryan faded into the background, walking over to the sidewalk to sit on a bench, letting the sheriff and his co-workers handle the worried parents and the clean-up of the scene. The cold air was adding to the stiffness creeping into his shoulders and neck. Finally, the sheriff walked over to him.

"The girls are shaken up but okay," said Jeff. "They both admit they were messing with the CDs and not paying attention to the road. I'll get the report typed up this afternoon, and you can pick up a copy tomorrow."

Ryan looked grimly at damage to the front quarter panel of his car as he listened.

Jeff closed his notepad. "Parents say they have insurance, so this should be pretty simple."

Ryan raised his eyebrows and met the man's gaze.

Jeff looked at the prized Fastback. "I'm guessing you're not going to take that to a shop."

Still looking at him, Ryan crossed his arms over his chest. "No."

"Want some help pounding that out?"

Ryan stood from the bench. "No."

"Come on. You know you hate body work."

"You are a good sheriff, Jeff, but a lousy mechanic."

"But this is just pounding out dents, right?" said Jeff, holding his hands out expressively toward the Mustang.

"I've seen your work with a hammer." Ryan started to walk away.

"One little mistake," Jeff muttered.

Ryan stopped and turned partially back, pointing at Jeff. "You broke your thumb."

"But it healed!" To prove his point, Jeff held up his left hand and wiggled his thumb.

Ryan grinned, shaking his head at the man's enthusiasm. Jeff was great at dealing with people but all thumbs with the most basic tools. "You can bring the pizza, but I am not handing you a mallet."

Jeff smiled broadly and called after him. "Just tell me your favorite soda and when you're going to work on it."

Ryan checked to make sure the wheel well was clear of the tire. Then he started his car and headed onto the fire station. He parked toward the back of the lot and walked up to the open door of his boss's office. "Hey, Isaac."

"Griffin. I was beginning to think you weren't coming back. I heard about the fender bender. You okay?"

"Yeah. Starting to get a little stiff, but not too bad."

"Good. You ready to get back to work?"

Isaac Betton liked to get straight to the point.

Ryan sat down in the chair across from Isaac. "Well, sir, I've been thinking about going back to school."

Isaac leaned back in his chair. "Haven't you been taking classes the whole time you've been here?"

"Yes, sir. I have. But I was thinking about switching my focus just a bit."

Ryan took a deep breath and tried to explain it the best he could. "My parents moved to a pretty small town about forty-five minutes south of Portland. Their medical care is a bit lacking."

"Small town, huh," Isaac nodded. "Ambulance service from Portland?"

"Yes, sir. Just a small clinic with rotating doctors."

"You thinking about going to school to be a doctor?"

"Leaning more towards a physician's assistant."

Isaac looked at him for a moment. Ryan often had trouble reading the man. In his mid-fifties, Isaac had grown up at the firehouse with his fire chief dad. Oregon was in the man's blood, and he could read people better than anyone Ryan had ever met.

Finally, Isaac nodded his head. "You'd be good at either. You have a personality that's good with people, the instincts that make you great at triage, and a calmness under pressure and critical care. But I have another option for you to think about." Isaac sat forward in his chair and leaned his arms on the desk. "Holmes just let me know he's going to be retiring. I'll need a lead paramedic and was considering you."

Ryan sat back, placing his right ankle on his left knee. He struggled to control his enthusiasm in front of his boss. "I appreciate that."

They talked more about the specifics of the job, the added responsibilities, and the small increase in pay. "I'll need a decision before the end of February."

"Understood, sir." Ryan stood to leave.

"And Griffin," said Isaac.

Ryan paused in the doorway.

"If you're determined to head back to school, let me know. With all the classes you've taken since you got your EMT associate's, I'm thinking you should be close to the medical school's prerequisite bachelor degree."

Isaac paused, and Ryan watched him, wondering where his boss was heading with all this. He waited patiently, leaning a shoulder against the doorjamb.

Finally Isaac continued. "I've got an old friend who works with the hiring department at Oregon Health & Science in Portland. I imagine that's the hospital sponsoring the clinic in your parents' town, and they are always looking for people willing to move to those small towns instead of forcing their doctors to rotate through."

Ryan was shocked. *He just offered me a job here—and then offered me an introduction into one in Portland?*

"I'm not sure what to say," said Ryan.

"Just let me know your decision within the month."

Chapter 18

THREE WEEKS LATER, BRITTNEY HUMMED as she updated her computer notes on her patients.

"My, my, aren't we in a pleasant mood," said Nicole, pulling her hair back into a ponytail. "Let's see. It's been a week since your Valentine flowers arrived from Ryan. Has he done something else?"

Brittney looked up from her screen. "It's because you are here to relieve me, and I have the next four days off!"

"Yeah, that and Romeo is meeting her for dinner tonight at Romano's," said Jennifer, winking at Nicole.

"So when is he moving to Portland?" asked Nicole.

"Why would you think he's moving here?" said Brittney.

"Crossing," corrected Jennifer with confidence.

"He's moving to Crossing?" said Nicole, her eyebrows disappearing into her bangs. "Isn't that where Dr. Williams is moving to, as well?" said Nicole.

"He hasn't said anything yet about moving," said Brittney.

"Then why is he coming to Portland?" said Nicole.

"We're all meeting in Crossing tomorrow for Amber's

birthday party," said Brittney absently while finalizing a note in her computer.

"I'm so confused," said Nicole. "He's driving from McWilliam to Portland so you two can go to Crossing tomorrow?"

"Uh-huh," said Brittney as she logged out.

"Sounds fishy to me," said Jennifer.

Puzzled, Brittney looked from one friend's face to the other. "What? We're taking Pops too."

Nicole rolled her eyes. "That's like driving from here to Seattle by way of California! Driving out of his way to see you one day earlier than he already was going to, sending flowers on significant holidays, text messages all day, regular e-mails, and phone calls." Nicole kept track of the list on her fingers. "He's got to have moving on the mind."

Brittney shook her head. "Look, last I heard, he hadn't made a decision on the job in McWilliam. It's a pretty important promotion."

"But McWilliam is twice as far away as Crossing," Jennifer pointed out.

"Would you leave us?" asked Nicole, looking at Brittney.

"Leave?" Surprise colored Brittney's face. "Where would I go?"

"Crossing!" said Nicole.

Brittney rubbed her temple. "How'd we get to me moving to Crossing?"

"Duh! Romeo…" said Jennifer, rolling her eyes and leaving the rest unspoken.

"Let's assume Ryan moves to Crossing to work with Dr. Williams," said Nicole leaning on the counter. "You have a really cute guy who is spending an awful lot of time keeping up with you and a really good doctor that you know running a clinic that will be in need of a nurse."

Transfer to the Crossing clinic? The possibility hit Brittney like a snowy avalanche, and an ideal image of her married to Ryan and working side by side with him popped into her head.

"You always did like working with Dr. Williams," Nicole reminded her.

"And then there's Romeo..." said Jennifer, waggling her eyebrows dramatically.

Brittney looked from Nicole to Jennifer. *Transfer? Could I? Ryan and I have been spending a lot of time talking, but he hasn't said anything about a future together. He's not said anything about the future other than his own career decisions.*

"Did Melody ever get a hold of you?" said Nicole, changing the subject.

Brittney closed out her notes as she thought about the last time she'd talked to the unit secretary. "No, why?"

"Just something odd," said Nicole with a slight frown.

"What?" Brittney saved her work and logged out of her workstation.

"Stephanie Malone's been sniffing around," said Nicole. She made a face.

Jennifer caught the name and immediately moved closer again. "What'd she want?"

"Who cares what she wants?" said Brittney.

"Melody wasn't sure what she was up to, but she was asking a lot of questions about you," said Nicole.

"Me?" said Brittney. "What kind of questions?"

"What kind of nurse are you, do you forget to log things in, how do you interact with the parents. Things like that."

Jennifer's eyes went wide. "Why's she going after you?"

Brittney thought back to the day she'd been talking to Ryan near the front entrance to the hospital.

"Melody said she thought she saw her talking with some of the parents too," Nicole added.

"Storm's brewing on the horizon," said Jennifer with a shake of her head.

"Well, not much I can do except my best on the job and wait for her to let me in on the unofficial inquiry," said Brittney. She shrugged, trying to convince herself Stephanie's questions weren't bothering her.

"I suppose," said Nicole slowly. "Well, I don't know what time you're meeting Ryan, but traffic's bad out there tonight. Want to update me on the kids so you can get out of here?"

"Umm, yeah," said Brittney, shaking off her worries. "Sure."

"You seem distracted tonight," said Ryan. He shifted in the bench seat of their table at the restaurant, quiet music playing in the background.

"Huh?" said Brittney, lost in her private concerns. "Oh, sorry. I am."

"What's going on?"

Brittney fiddled with her napkin and sat up straighter, glancing quickly around for the waitress. "I just—I don't know. A couple things, I guess," she said, her gaze returning to the napkin in her hands. "Do you think it's going to be much longer for our food?"

"Don't change the subject."

"I'm not. I'm just hungry."

"Uh-huh. Are you going to actually tell me anything, or are you going to keep talking to your napkin?"

Her eyes flew to his face, and she dropped the napkin on the table. "Well, I'm not sure how to...I'm not sure what...I don't think..."

Ryan reached out and covered Brittney's hands with his own. "Stop. Breathe."

A tingle raced up her arms. Ryan touching her hands was not helping her to think more clearly. She took a slow, deep breath.

"Now quit avoiding whatever it is you don't want to bring up, and let's get it out between us," said Ryan. "You aren't even looking at me tonight. Did I do something to irritate you?"

She looked at him for a moment and saw concern in his eyes. "No, you haven't done anything wrong. An idea was presented to me earlier today that I hadn't thought about before. But it also brought up other questions."

"Okay..." said Ryan.

Brittney slouched back in her seat, removing her hands from Ryan's. "You've been talking about your job choices. Have you made a decision yet?"

Ryan twisted slightly in the seat and put his arm along the top of the bench. "I did talk to an advisor at the university. She said that I basically just need a couple more sciences, statistics, and one more humanities class to get my bachelor's and be able to apply to the medical school."

Brittney frowned. "That would be a pretty heavy load for one semester."

"Especially while working. I think I could knock one class out this summer, then a couple this fall and one in the spring to finish it up."

Brittney took a deep breath and then asked the question that had weighed so heavily on her mind. "So are you going to take the promotion in McWilliam?"

Suddenly, their waitress was at the table. "Here's your pepperoni pizza. Please be careful. The pan is very hot." She set the pizza down between them. "Can I get you anything else?"

"I think we're fine," said Ryan with a smile.

Brittney waited, tension building in her neck and shoulders.

Ryan served a slice onto her plate. "Want to pray so we can eat while we keep talking?"

Brittney shrugged her shoulders, willing the tension to leave them. "Whatever."

Ryan paused in the middle of grabbing a slice for his own plate. "Whatever?"

Ashamed of the way she was acting, Brittney took a deep breath. "Sorry. I didn't mean it the way it sounded. I just worked four days in a row, and I'm exhausted and not good company. Maybe it would be better if I just went home."

Ryan looked critically at her. "I don't buy it."

"What?"

"You, my dear, are a lying chicken."

Brittney started to open her mouth but then closed it abruptly. She closed her eyes and rubbed her temples. *He's right. I am lying, and tonight I am definitely a chicken.*

"So, do my career plans have something to do with your distracted mind?"

Brittney wasn't sure how to answer that question safely. Everything she thought to say led back to her wondering if she and Ryan were just friends, or if they were working on more than that.

"How about this," said Ryan as steam from the fresh pizza rose between them. "Since we're all expected in Crossing tomorrow for Rachel-Amber's birthday party, I'll pick up Pops in the morning. Then we'll swing by your place to get you. I don't see any reason why we should both drive."

"Okay." She opened her eyes and looked across the table at him, grateful for the change in conversation. "Truce."

He looked at her and nodded. He picked up a piece of pizza—the melted cheese stretching before breaking free from the pie—and laid it on his plate.

"I told Pops I would pick him up around nine in the morning. But riding in my car would be easier for Pops than your Mustang."

"So we switch tonight." He shrugged as he took a bite.

"We switch what?"

"Vehicles."

Brittney's eyes were huge. *His prized '68 Mustang? He's going to just hand me the keys?* "You're going to drive my Equinox home and let me take your Mustang?"

"Why not? You can drive a stick shift, can't you?"

"It's been a while, but yeah. I just didn't think you'd ever let anyone else drive that car."

"Mom and Dad can't drive a stick, and Keith's not going near it for several more years." He took a drink. "Kinda got the impression Pete would like to, but he hasn't asked."

Brittney picked up her pizza, feeling a little better. "Okay, deal. We switch vehicles tonight, and I'll be ready to go by nine-fifteen."

Chapter 19

RYAN KNOCKED ON POPS' FRONT door at 8:55 the next morning.

"Morning, sir."

Pops looked him over and glanced at a clock hanging in the hall. "Early, huh. Like that."

Pops stepped back to a small table to grab his keys and then picked up his coat from a nearby chair. Ryan saw an overnight bag sitting near the door. "Can I carry your bag to the car?"

"Yep. That'd be fine."

As they walked out to Brittney's car, Pops said, "Just what are your intentions, young man?"

Intentions? "Well, sir. Today my intentions are to get you and your granddaughter safely to Crossing for my sister's birthday party." Ryan put the bag in the back of the car and looked at Pops.

"Yeah. And tomorrow?"

"I would have to say my intentions tomorrow are to return you both safely home again."

"Blast it, boy. Are you always this irritating?"

"Probably, sir," said Ryan with a grin, leaning on the side of the car. "At least when the intent of the questioner is unclear."

Pops took a step closer and pointed in Ryan's face. "What are your intentions with my granddaughter?"

The grin left Ryan's face. He knew this man could help or hinder his hopes with Brittney. He wanted the old man on his side. He'd hoped to have part of this conversation with Brittney last night, but whatever had been on her mind hadn't given him the impression that it would have gone well.

"Honestly, sir, my intent is to take a job at the Crossing clinic and convince your granddaughter to transfer to the nursing job so she can work alongside me—as my wife." *Did I just say that out loud?*

Pops looked at him intently, and Ryan didn't relax during the scrutiny. Pops finally nodded. "Good." He turned and opened his door. "Saves me the trouble of pushing you two together all weekend."

Shocked, Ryan watched him climb into the car and shut his door. He grinned as he walked around to his own door. *One man of the family down, three to go.*

The short trip to Brittney's was uneventful, and they quickly picked up the two-lane highway south. A few miles outside of town, they came across a line of stopped traffic.

"Wonder what's up?" said Brittney, glancing around.

Ryan tried to look ahead but couldn't see anything except the line of vehicles.

"Probably an accident," said Pops. "Always stupid people driving this road like it's the autobahn. Particularly dangerous in late February!"

"Brittney," said Ryan. "Why don't you move up here? I'm going to walk down and see if anyone needs help." Ryan got out of the car and held the door for her to switch from the back seat to the front. "Keep your cell phone close."

Ryan zipped up his coat and jogged down the line of cars until he saw the accident scene and other people standing around. "Has anyone called 9-1-1?"

"I did," said a woman standing nearby.

He quickly assessed the situation. *One car upside down in the ditch, probably totaled, with at least one passenger inside. One lady hysterical on the outside of the car trying to get in. Another car fairly crunched in the middle of the road with at least one person inside.*

He looked around and pointed to a man nearby. "Sir, I need you to start working with the drivers of these cars to clear a working area for the emergency vehicles coming from Portland."

Then he looked back to the woman who said she called 9-1-1. "Ma'am, I need you to tell the drivers on the other side that they might want to turn around and find another road."

He pulled his cell phone from his pocket and called Brittney. "I need you to pull the car as far off the road as you safely can and call 9-1-1 to give them an update on the accident on Highway 26. A lady says she's already called, but tell them it's a two-car accident with multiple injuries. We'll need fire and rescue, maybe jaws of life. Also tell them a paramedic and nurse are on the scene, and then I need you to hurry down here to help me."

He shut the phone and went to the car in the middle of the road first. "Sir, can you hear me?" The man looked at Ryan, very dazed. "Can you hear me?"

He slowly nodded.

"Does anything hurt?" The man stared at him at him for a moment and then looked back out the windshield.

Ryan did a quick check. *Conscious, but probably in deep shock. Breathing, seatbelt on, no obvious signs of bleeding.* Ryan touched the man's hands that still held the steering wheel, noting both felt warm to the touch. He looked around again and caught the attention of another onlooker. "Sir, I need your help."

The man strode forward, eager to help. "This man seems to be okay, just in shock. I need you to stay here with him and try to get him to talk to you. Look in the glove box and see if you can find a name or address or something to see if that helps him refocus. Just don't leave him until the paramedics get here. Let me know if he loses consciousness or you start seeing any blood."

Ryan jogged over to the hysterical woman, the sound of a crying baby getting closer. "Ma'am."

"My baby!" She grabbed Ryan's sleeve and pulled him toward the car.

"Ma'am!" He grabbed both her arms. "I'll get your baby, but I need you to calm down." Ryan glanced her over and only saw minor cuts and a goose egg forming on her right temple.

"Please get my baby. Please…"

"How old?"

The woman tried pulling Ryan toward the car again. "Please, my baby!"

"Ma'am. How old is your baby?"

"She's five months. Please!"

"Okay. I'll get her. You stay up here for me."

Brittney came running up past all the stopped vehicles. "What do you need?"

"Stay with her. She seems coherent but has head trauma. I'm going to look closer at the car and see if I can get to the baby." Ryan carefully made his way down into the ditch and looked at the driver through a cracked front window. *Suspended in his seat belt, unconscious, bleeding, seems to be breathing, but tough to tell with jacket on.* He looked into the back seat, but the car was at a bad angle. He couldn't see the child, but from the sounds of the cries, he knew she was conscious and breathing without a problem. At least the car seat was still firmly attached to the back seat. He tried pushing on the car, stepping back as it moved.

He crawled back up out of the ditch and looked at Brittney. "The car's too unstable. I can't get in without putting the driver and child at further risk."

He looked at the cars closest to the accident. Many of the drivers were standing around, watching the drama unfold before them. He called out, "Does anyone have a jack in their car I can use? I need two or three."

Four drivers went to their trunks and pulled out what they had. One man climbed down in the ditch with Ryan and helped place the jacks in various positions, stabilizing the car enough for Ryan to get in the back seat through a broken window.

As he crawled into position, a small, red face looked down at him. "Hey, there, sweet girl." Ryan could finally hear the sound of sirens in the distance. He reached for the baby, and she started to whimper. He moved slightly to be able to catch her more easily once he released the straps holding her into the seat. "It's a good thing your momma made sure these straps were nice and tight around you, little one."

As the baby cried, he felt for broken bones or signs of bleeding. Not finding any obvious signs of injury, he reached up to release the latch. Just as he caught her, the car shifted in the snow. Hearing glass crunch under his shoulder, Ryan cuddled her close until the car settled. Carefully, he handed the baby out the window to his helper before crawling out himself.

"Get that baby up to the women, then help me tighten up these jacks."

He began checking the jacks closest to him, tightening one against the bank a little more. He looked at the man who'd been helping him. "Make sure you're up the ditch a bit in case this car shifts again. When Fire and Rescue get here, let them know that a paramedic is in the car and the driver is unconscious."

"Got it."

Ryan tested the car again before crawling in the back window, carefully moving toward the front seat. He pulled the man's coat open and saw rapid movement in his chest. *Okay. So you're breathing, but it's fast. What else is wrong with you?*

"What's the situation?" he heard from the road above.

"A paramedic went in the car after the driver who is unconscious," said Ryan's helper.

A moment later a fire fighter looked through the back window. "Sir? I'm with Gilbert Fire Station. What do you have?"

"Patient is unconscious with at least one broken leg and a fever," said Ryan. "Several minor scrapes and a decent laceration on his head, but I'm concerned about a punctured lung."

"Roger that." The man turned away from the vehicle. "Let's get this car secure and that door open!"

Ryan felt the first responders placing additional bracing to the car.

The fire fighter from Gilbert Station handed some items through the back window to Ryan. "Here's a neck collar for the victim and a coat to protect you while we get this door opened."

Ryan buckled the neck collar in place around the man and then held the fire coat around the man's face, letting it fall down along the door to protect them both while the firefighters worked to open the door.

"We're all set in here," Ryan yelled behind him.

A second fireman responded to Ryan from the front passenger door. "We're going to try to pry it open now."

He heard the man at the back window communicating Ryan's assessment to the waiting paramedic. In just a moment, the passenger side door was open. Ryan got out of the way while the first responders laid a backboard on the inside roof of the car, then helped support the unconscious man while the seatbelt was cut. The team laid him as gently as they could on the backboard before removing him from the vehicle.

Ryan climbed up the side of the ditch and surveyed the activity. One ambulance was preparing to pull away, while a fireman helped the woman and her baby into a second ambulance that waited for her husband. A wrecker stood by in the distance, ready to move close enough to begin hauling the mangled vehicles away.

"Name's Donovan," said the fireman Ryan had been talking to through the back window.

"Griffin," said Ryan. He shook the man's hand.

"Good work today. You assigned someplace around here?"

"I'm about to start working for Oregon Health and Science, assigned to the clinic in Crossing."

Donovan nodded. "You're welcome at Gilbert Station anytime. Feel free to seek some first aid at the truck."

Ryan looked at his hands and saw several nicks and spots of blood. His pants had definitely seen better days. "Thanks. We're not far from Crossing. I think I'll just head there."

Ryan strode over to Brittney. Pops had followed her to see the action firsthand.

"Impressive, young man." Pops turned to look at Brittney. "You should hang onto this one, girl."

Ryan grinned. "You guys wait here. I'll go get the car. The wrecker should have the road cleared soon."

Chapter 20

Brittney walked into her mom's kitchen with Ryan and Pops bringing up the rear. "We're here!"

"Oh, good!" said Faye, getting up from the table. "How is everyone?"

"Do you know how those involved in the accident are doing?" said Frank.

"The worst one was the guy stuck in the car," said Ryan, going to the sink to wash his hands. "He had a broken leg, probably a concussion, and a punctured lung."

"That woman had to be fine, the way she was carrying on," said Pops, shaking his head at the memory.

"You should have seen her before Ryan got the baby out," said Brittney.

"She was hysterical when I got on the scene," Ryan agreed.

"Mom, are your first aid supplies in the bathroom? Ryan needs some attention."

"Yes, in the medicine cabinet," said Faye, approaching Ryan to see what he needed.

Brittney found some antiseptic wash and gauze pads. Going

back to the kitchen, she looked at Ryan. "Come sit on a bar stool." She went to work on his hands first, then examined the rips in his pants for scrapes, working through the cuts in the material.

"Happy now?" he said as she stood, a look of amusement on his face.

She put the lid back on the antiseptic. "Better. Although when you take those pants off, you should probably use some more of this."

"Is anyone hungry?" said Faye.

"Yes," said Ryan, sliding off the bar stool.

"Boy earned his meal today," said Pops, taking a seat at the table, "crawling in and out of that car."

"How bad was the accident?" said Frank.

Faye started pulling out sandwich bread and lunch meats. Brittney joined her and began putting together sandwiches. Ryan took his place at the table.

"One car wasn't too bad, just banged up and sitting in the middle of the road," said Brittney.

"Other'n was upside down in the ditch," said Pops. "Boy had to secure it before he could get in it."

"Secure it?" said Faye, glancing over her shoulder. "How'd you do that?" She put a sandwich on a plate and handed it to Ryan.

"Thanks. You just put jacks in places where it doesn't have any support," said Ryan, setting the plate on his placemat. "Lots of onlookers, so a few pulled out their car jacks to help until Fire and Rescue arrived with theirs."

"I had no idea being a paramedic could be dangerous," said Faye, obviously impressed.

"It's not always," said Ryan dismissively.

"Want something to drink?" asked Faye.

"Water, please," said Ryan.

"Me, too," said Pops.

"Sure would be good to have someone like you down here in Crossing," said Frank meaningfully before taking a bite of his sandwich.

Ryan didn't say anything. He really wanted Brittney to know his decision before the rest of her family. Pops had surprised him into sharing his plan, but Ryan felt fairly certain the old man would keep that information to himself.

"John is moving down this weekend," said Faye as she and Brittney passed out the drinks and took their seats at the table. "I believe Allie said that they are expecting him and Micah for dinner tonight."

"Is that Dr. Williams?" said Ryan before sipping his water.

"Yes," said Faye. "He hasn't visited regularly in many years, but Micah is looking forward to him being here."

"Been thinkin' myself about moving down here," said Pops casually.

"Dad?" said Frank, nearly losing his grip on his sandwich.

"You're leaving Portland?" said Brittney.

"Think it's time I was closer," said Pops with a sideways glance toward Ryan. "Fresh air might do me good."

"Well, that's certainly something for us to think about," said Faye.

Brittney pushed back from the table. "I'm going to go put my bag upstairs. Want me to take yours too, Pops?"

Before he could answer, she grabbed both and hurried to her room. Sitting on the bed, her mind spun. *Father, I don't know what to think. Almost everyone will be living here. I don't see Logan moving back here, but he is on this side of Portland, not too far away. What do I do? Stay at Doernbecher? I don't know if my heart can take another case like Gracie, but I know it will come. Those sweet children will penetrate my defenses, and I will become emotionally attached to them. And I will lose some. What should I do? So much is changing. Is it time for another change?*

She thought of Ryan and how much her heart was getting tangled up in him. She looked forward to his e-mails, and a text in the middle of the day always brought a smile to her face. *But he hasn't said he's moving. And what if he does take the job, but the hospital doesn't assign him to Crossing? It would be nice to work with Dr. Williams. But if I move here and then Ryan ends up in Portland... And lest I forget, Ryan has yet to declare his undying love for me...*

Brittney sighed and walked over to the dresser. She looked at her anxious reflection in the mirror. "I'm talking myself in circles. I need to have this conversation with Ryan, not myself."

She tucked a lock of hair behind her ear and walked back downstairs.

"Brittney!"

Amber waited at the bottom of the stairs for Brittney to descend, and then she enveloped her in a hug.

"Hey, Amber! You're back! How's it going?"

"Better than I dreamed," Amber gushed. "How about you? I was sorry to hear about Grace passing away."

"Yeah, that was tough. But the kids I'm working with now

look good. Joshua especially is responding very well to treatment. I think he's going to be home in record time if he keeps progressing like he has been."

"That's great."

The door to the mudroom opened, and Peter stepped inside with Ryan. "Look who I found wandering around outside," said Peter to Amber.

Amber slipped back into the kitchen to give her brother a warm hug. Brittney followed but hung back slightly.

"Apparently he's turning into quite the local hero," said Peter.

"Doing what?" Amber asked.

"We ran into a bad car accident coming down this morning. Ryan managed the scene and began triage until fire and rescue got there," Brittney explained with obvious pride for Ryan's skills.

"Wow," said Amber. "I'm impressed. Do Mom and Dad know yet?"

"I was just doing my job." Ryan waved his hand dismissively. "Not a big deal."

"Which might have saved one man's life. Not sure I can boast so much from my job." Peter clapped Ryan on the shoulder.

"So what's the plan for tonight?" said Ryan, changing the subject.

"No emergencies," said Amber decisively.

"I could go for that!" said Brittney. She wrapped her arm around Amber. They strolled into the living room and sat on the couch, leaving Peter and Ryan behind to discuss the repairs to the Mustang from the accident in McWilliam.

"So what's really going on?" Amber shifted so she was facing Brittney.

"What do you mean?"

"Your mind is on something."

Brittney laid back and put her head on the back of the couch. She focused on the snowy mountain peaks outside the windows. "Well, one thing is Stephanie Malone."

"Why is she bugging you?"

"I'm not sure. She irritated me a few weeks back. It was right after Gracie. Ryan and I were going up to see Josh. He got to the front entrance before me, and when I walked in, I saw her fawning all over him."

"I'm not sure I would have handled that well," said Amber, clearly remembering her own experiences with Stephanie.

"I didn't. I never liked her, even before you came along! I sauntered over and gave her the impression that Ryan and I were together. And then I rubbed your marriage in her face."

Amber pulled both legs up, wrapping her arms around them. "Oh! I would have paid to see that!"

"Yeah, well apparently since then, she's been snooping around, asking questions about me at work."

"What kind of questions?"

"The kind that make it seem like she's trying to get me into trouble."

"Can she do that?"

"Well, it would probably be hard. She is on the board in her father's place, but normally for a nurse to get called before the board you have to be having doctor issues. I don't think my supervisor would give her two minutes, but the HR department? I don't know." Brittney sighed deeply and put her hair behind an ear.

"So what else is going on?"

Brittney took a deep breath. She and Amber had talked many hours about all kinds of things, but Amber had usually been the one opening her heart. Not Brittney. "Some friends at worked thought I'd be moving down here soon," Brittney finally admitted.

Amber's eyes lit up. "Why would they think that?"

Brittney grabbed the pillow on the couch beside her and hugged it tight. She looked at Amber and watched Amber's eyes look toward the people still having a conversation in the kitchen.

"Ryan?" said Amber quietly. "Do they think he's going to take the job in Crossing, and so they expect you to move down here with him?"

Brittney closed her eyes for a moment, unsure of how much of her heart she really wanted to expose to Ryan's sister.

Amber laid a hand on Brittney's arm. "Do you like Ryan?"

She looked at Amber. "As a friend? Yes," she hedged.

"You know what I meant," Amber said with a hint of impatience and a poke in the arm.

"As more than a friend?" Brittney shrugged self-consciously. "I don't know."

"How long have you not known?"

Brittney looked at Amber and answered slowly. "Since about

the wedding. I think. Maybe." Brittney sighed and laid her head on the back of the couch. "I'm doing it again."

"Doing what?"

"It seems like every time I start thinking about life with him, or the possibility of life with him, I start talking in three and four-word sentences. It's like I can't put a coherent thought together."

"Sounds like you get flustered thinking about it." Amber grinned knowingly.

"Maybe so." Brittney glanced at her face. "What are you grinning about?"

"We could be double-related soon!"

"Now you're jumping way ahead."

"Jumping ahead of what?" said Peter, ambling into the room with Ryan behind him.

Brittney and Amber looked at each other. "Nothing!" they said together, breaking out in giggles.

Chapter 21

ALITTLE BEFORE DINNER, RYAN PULLED Brittney off the couch. "Come on," he said. "Let's go for a walk."

They stopped in the kitchen long enough to let Faye know they'd be back soon before grabbing coats from the mudroom and heading out. Brittney picked a well-worn path through the trees that led to the river.

"So, I wanted you to know before it comes out at dinner tonight that I've made a decision."

Brittney walked quietly beside him, seemingly focusing on the trail.

"I turned down the job in McWilliam."

Brittney stopped in the path and looked at him. "Oh," she finally said, releasing her breath. "I'm not sure I expected that."

"Well, in the short-term, the money would have been better, and the experience would have looked great on my resume." Ryan grabbed her hand and turned her so they could continue down the path.

"So why turn it down?"

Ryan glanced at her from the corner of his eye. "Because I'm slowly learning to look a little farther than the near future. And I'm beginning to see greater value in some intangibles."

"Intangibles?"

They reached the edge of the river, and he looked appreciatively at the flowing water and the sturdy firs along the bank. "Things like having time to relax with family, forming relationships that last."

He turned and looked directly at her. "Love and family have definitely moved way up on my priority list over the last couple of months."

He looked for something in her eyes that would give him the courage to proceed, but he saw conflict. He'd sensed she was holding something back since their dinner at Romano's last night, but he couldn't tell if it had to do with him or not. Hope of a life with her fought to survive.

She turned from him and stepped closer to the river, seemingly fascinated by the small branch that was floating past. "So does that mean you're going to try to get the job in Crossing?"

Ryan stood behind her, uncertain. "I've already talked to my boss's contact in human resources. He's sending my application packet through the proper channels, but he doesn't think it will be a problem. He's trying to rush it so Dr. Williams won't be on his own for too long."

He waited quietly. *Come on, B. Deflect or change the topic. Give me the sign that this is important to you, that this hits close to your heart and you don't want to talk about it.*

She appeared to be looking upstream, staring off into space. Finally, she turned around as if she had come to a decision.

"Come on, I'll show you my mom's favorite spot not too far from here."

Ryan suppressed a grin as she pulled him along the path and continued talking.

"How are the repairs to your Mustang going? I saw it was covered in primer. Does that mean it just needs painted now?"

Two weeks later, Ryan pulled into Frank and Faye's driveway as the evening stars began to appear overhead. The night was clear and slightly warmer than normal for early March.

After parking in front of the garage, he made his way to the porch. He took a deep breath and knocked on the front door.

"Ryan!" said Faye as the door swung open. "This is a surprise. Come on in! What are you doing here?"

Ryan wiped his shoes on the welcome mat and stepped inside. "I'm hoping to catch you and Frank alone. I need to talk to you."

"Of course, dear. Come on in." Faye closed the door behind him and led the way into the living room. Frank was comfortably seated in a chair with a book. He stood when Ryan walked into the room.

"Ryan. Good to see you."

"Thank you, sir. I was hoping you'd be home tonight," said Ryan.

"We're usually home," said Frank. "You just never know how many will be here with us!" He winked at his wife.

"Now, you talk like I have people over all the time," said

Faye, pretending to be offended.

"Quite frequently, love. Not that I'm complaining, mind you."

"Ryan, I'm sure you don't want to talk about all this," said Faye. "Sit down. Tell us what's on your mind." Faye sat down on the couch nearest Frank, allowing Ryan the chair where he'd be able to face them both at the same time.

"Well, as you know, I'll be starting to work at the clinic in a couple weeks with Dr. Williams."

"We're all very excited about that," said Faye with a nod.

"I plan to maintain my paramedic license for now. But I've already started the enrollment process at the university so I can finish my bachelor's and then work towards a physician's assistant."

"What's that?" said Frank. "Is that like a nurse?"

"Not really. It's more like a doctor, but it's less school. I'll still have to work under a licensed M.D., but I'll be able to do pretty much everything Dr. Williams can do, except for surgery."

"That sounds wonderful, dear," said Faye, tilting her head and waiting for more.

"With Dr. Williams and I, plus Betsy at the front desk, that almost fully staffs the clinic on a regular basis. Everyone lives in Crossing, so medical care should improve drastically. The only thing we'll be missing is a regular nurse."

"Well, that all sounds pretty good. Certainly better than we've had in a long time." said Faye.

"Yes, ma'am." Ryan looked at Frank.

"Have you decided where you're going to live?" said Faye.

Frank covered Faye's hand with his own. "Love, I think the boy has more to say."

Keeping his eyes steady on Frank, Ryan said, "I'd like to encourage Brittney to ask for a transfer to the clinic." Ryan swallowed. "I'd also like your permission and blessing to ask Brittney to become my wife."

Faye gasped, putting one hand up to her mouth. "Oh, Ryan, dear."

Ryan remained focused on Frank's eyes. *It's all out in the open. All my plans. Frank, say something.*

"I've been watching you, son, ever since you first came here," said Frank. "You seemed to be sittin' the fence, not sure whether or not you liked God's path."

"That's true."

"Has that changed?"

"Honestly, yes. When I first came here, I watched everyone a lot. As I watched my sister and saw how much she was learning to trust God, it made me realize that He was only God to me, some figurehead in the sky watching to see how closely I followed the rules. I didn't really want to get close to Him if that's all He was. But as I've been here, as I've watched you and learned more of the history of this family, I discovered that you believe in more than I dreamed was possible. That your God not only wanted a relationship with me, but that He might actually be pursuing me. So, I put Him to the test."

"A test?" said Faye.

"Yes, much like Gideon in the Bible," said Ryan. "I asked for clear direction in my career. And things began falling into place. Within a week, I'd become aware of the issues at the clinic and been given the opportunity to help both Eleni and Billy with non-emergency conditions. And Brittney, not fully knowing what was going on in my head, suggested I go back to school to become a doctor."

"Gideon didn't exactly ask for clear direction in his career, son," said Frank.

"No, sir. He didn't," said Ryan.

"Then why focus on Gideon?" said Frank.

Ryan looked down at his hands for a moment, then back at Frank. "I hesitate to tell you because I just... I'm not quite sure how to explain it."

"Try us," said Faye.

Ryan took a deep breath. *This is a huge risk.* "The morning of my sister's wedding, I... well, to be truthful, I don't really know what it was. At the time, I thought I was awake, but when it was over, I woke up. So maybe it was a dream."

He paused and looked at Frank and Faye. Both were paying close attention. *Well, that's good. I haven't freaked them out yet.*

"In this dream, or whatever it was, a man stood by my bedroom door. He said that I was being sent. He said that I've been made for more than I've taken hold of. Then he told me to read Judges six through seven so I'd know what God does for those who obey."

"You saw an angel?" said Faye. She looked at Frank.

"He didn't happen to have blond hair and blue eyes," said Frank. "Dressed in blue jeans and hiking boots?"

Ryan's jaw dropped. He stared at Frank in disbelief. "How'd you know that?" said Ryan.

"Peter's seen him," said Frank.

"The morning of the wedding?" said Ryan, still slack-jawed.

"No, just before Christmas," said Faye. "And just after Christmas, Andy talked to him."

"His name's Matthew," said Frank by way of explanation.

"Yeah, he did say that." Ryan stood and paced over to the hearth, rubbing his jaw. *An angel?* Ryan had considered the possibility, but to say it out loud seemed ludicrous. *Since when do angels talk to humans? Sure, the stories in the Bible, but... modern America?*

"Do you know what he was trying to tell you?" said Faye.

Ryan turned to face her. "I think so. He, uh, Matthew, said something I didn't understand at the time. He said, 'Being sent does not necessarily mean a change in location. Sometimes it simply refers to a destination.'"

Ryan sat down on the ottoman and rubbed his knuckles. "I realized that in my own way, I've been running just as much as my sister had been. I stayed in contact with my family, but I didn't support them much in their search for her, and I certainly didn't spend a lot time with them—like Christmas. I'd use any excuse to not be with them, even for holidays."

Ryan rubbed his jaw. He told himself that he'd already shared so much with Frank and Faye that continuing wouldn't cost him too much more. "I also changed jobs every time a co-worker wanted to get close. It didn't matter whether they wanted to meet for coffee or have me over for a barbeque. I didn't want to take the risk of being hurt again like when Amber left home."

"So now you're moving to Crossing and determined to stay put?" said Faye.

"Yes, ma'am," said Ryan. "I don't know if Brittney said

anything, but I had the option to stay in McWilliam and take a promotion. I turned my boss down. Whether Brittney agrees to move here or not, I've made my decision. I know I've still got a long way to go with God, but I know that Crossing is where God wants me."

"You've come a long way, son," said Frank. He paused, looking at Faye before continuing. She nodded her agreement, and he looked back at Ryan. "It'd be my honor if you'd get that girl of mine to say yes to marriage."

Ryan beamed. He stood to offer his hand to Frank. "Thank you, sir. Thank you."

Chapter 22

"MORNING, NICOLE," SAID BRITTNEY AS she arrived at the nurses' station. "How'd the night go?"

"Good. Everyone's looking great this morning. Dr. Vanwert wants a call once the morning labs are back on Joshua."

"Okay. Did Lori sleep through the night?"

"Pretty close. She got about six hours in, much better than the last three nights."

"Awesome. Sounds like we're through the worst of it until her next dose of chemo Tuesday."

Brittney logged onto the computer and checked emails while Nicole finished making her notes.

"Morning, Brittney!"

Brittney looked up from her computer to see Melody walking towards her. "Hey, girl! How's that Army man of yours?"

"He's good. He's preparing to deploy right now, so I don't expect to see him for awhile. He's going to try to get down here one more time before they leave, but you never know with the Army, right?"

"I suppose." Brittney looked at the girl, wondering how it

would feel to watch the man she loved go off to war.

"Anyway, I came out to tell you that Dr. Goldner wants to see you a.s.a.p."

"Dr. Goldner? Did she say why?"

"Nope. She just called and asked me to pass on the message. Said sooner was better than later."

"Okay. Thanks, Mel." *Why would one of the top doctors in the hospital want to see me? She's not part of Joshua's or Lori's care teams.* "Nicole, you got a few to hang out while I go track her down this morning?"

"Sure. As long as you bring me something chocolate on your way back."

"Deal."

Brittney walked over to Dr. Meggan Goldner's office in the main hospital. She knocked on the open door, noticing the simple, muted décor. The hospital's soft green walls were accented in Dr. Goldner's office with grey furniture and black and white framed prints on the wall. The otherwise depressing room was brightened with the occasional burst of bright yellow through the pillows and wall clock.

"Ma'am, you wanted to see me?"

"Brittney Yager?" said Dr. Goldner, looking up from her computer.

"Yes, ma'am," said Brittney.

"Please, come sit down."

Brittney sat in a comfortable grey and white plaid chair. Dr. Goldner sat back in her office chair.

"I wanted us to talk before anyone else got to you. I don't

know how much you may have heard already, but someone is trying to make trouble for you."

Brittney had not expected to hear that from the doctor. "Trouble for me? Why?"

"Well, I'm not exactly sure. I'll be honest enough to tell you that I've made some quiet inquiries, and I'm impressed with all I'm hearing. Your peers find you compassionate and well qualified. Your employment record shows no sign of discord among patients or supervisors. And a couple parents I talked to bubbled with enthusiasm about the difference you've made to their understanding of their child's treatment and prognosis."

"Thank you. But I don't understand. If everyone's happy with my performance, then who's causing problems?"

"I'm hoping you can spread some light on that. The person is Stephanie Malone."

Understanding flooded through Brittney. She immediately stood and walked to the window overlooking one of the parking lots.

"I take it you know her?" said Dr. Goldner.

"That woman is a walking drama camp," said Brittney. She clenched her fists, striving to keep her emotions in check. She turned and looked back at Dr. Goldner. "Can I be honest?"

"Please do."

"My brother used to drive to Portland about a once a week from Crossing where he and our parents live. He would typically meet Stephanie somewhere for dinner or a show. I never liked her, but they'd met in college, and he was trying to redeem her or some such nonsense."

"So what happened?"

"He broke it off and married someone else a little over a month ago."

"So she's striking out at you to get back at him?"

Brittney groaned, walking back to her chair to slouch down in it. "I don't know. Maybe. But, that's not all. Just after the wedding, I ran into her here at the hospital and may have sort of rubbed my brother's wedding in her face."

"I imagine she didn't take that well."

"You could say that. I should have handled myself better."

"Look, I'm sure you realize that it's very unusual for the board to consider anything related to a member of the nursing staff like this. In my opinion, you've done nothing to warrant scrutiny. But she's powerful, or rather her father is, and I don't know that she'll let this drop."

"So what do you recommend?"

"You could stay and fight through this here. I don't believe anyone on the board is currently taking this seriously. But it could be some pretty rough weather for a while."

"And if I don't like that option?"

"Transfer within the hospital system. If you're not working here at the main hospital, you two won't see each other. Out of sight, out of mind, one might hope."

Brittney thought about the kids she'd be leaving behind. "I've worked with cancer kids since I graduated."

"How long ago was that?"

"Four years."

"It definitely takes a specially blessed nurse to work with kids, doubly blessed to work with cancer patients. I find doctors and nurses who work in tough areas like that tend to have such a huge heart for it that they sometimes overlook their own care. You may be doing fine, but if you have it, why not take a couple days leave and think about all this? If you stay to fight, you'll need the strength that the rest will provide. But maybe you will find that a transfer would be better all the way around."

"You think I should leave?"

"Brittney, from your reputation, I think the hospital would be losing a great asset if you choose to transfer out. But I fear that the hospital will do you a great injustice if you stay. I'm not saying quit. I'm forewarning you so you can weigh the costs."

"Thank you, Dr. Goldner."

"Take care, Brittney."

As she left the office, Brittney headed straight to the coffee kiosk and purchased two large hot chocolates, one to fulfill her promise to Nicole and one to soothe her own ruffled nerves.

Brittney watched Ryan pull in beside her Equinox. When he cut his engine, she stepped out. Although the afternoon temperatures reached into the mid-fifties, the sun's strength was fading.

"This is where you want to spend your lunchbreak?" said Ryan with a glance around at the scenery.

"I'm not really hungry," said Brittney. She led the way down the pathway on the Westside Trail in Portland's metropolitan area.

"You, not hungry? What's up?"

"Why does something have to be up?" She shrugged and kept walking. "I needed the exercise, and this is close to work." She stuffed her hands into her coat pockets.

"Okay, lyin' chicken."

She stopped abruptly and looked at him. So many hateful thoughts flowed through her mind that it was stunning. "Look, just because I don't choose to tell you everything doesn't mean I'm lying!"

"Agreed. But don't avoid or deflect. You hate it when I do that, and you call me on it," Ryan said reasonably. "I'm just asking that you apply the same standard to yourself. You don't want to talk about it, just say so and I'll lay off."

Brittney stared at Ryan for a moment, then turned away. *He's not done anything except meet me out here on a cold trail in March. It's not his fault I'm being targeted.* She sighed deeply and turned back around.

"You're right. I was deflecting, and I'm sorry. I just have to make a hard decision about work."

As they walked, passing bare oaks and tall pines, Brittney poured out the whole story from the meeting with Dr. Goldner and her guilt over pushing Stephanie's buttons.

"I ran into her at the hospital yesterday," said Ryan.

Brittney clenched her fists and pushed them into her jacket pockets. "Yeah?"

"She was just telling me that some are excited about Dr. Williams and I moving to Crossing."

"Why would she bother to tell you that?"

Ryan shrugged. "Just to have a conversation, I suppose."

"She's chasing you," said Brittney ground out. A twig snapped underfoot.

Ryan stopped walking and folded his arms across his chest. "Are you jealous?"

Brittney tried to keep walking, but Ryan strode forward and grabbed her arm.

"Are you jealous?" he repeated.

Brittney thought about lying, thought about deflecting. But something in his eyes pulled the truth from her. "Yes, I was jealous."

He smiled at her, and Brittney could almost see his ego inflating three sizes. "Now if you're going to get all big-headed…"

He took a step toward her. "I'm not getting big-headed."

She tilted her head and squinted one eye, smiling back at him.

"Okay, maybe a little." He grinned broadly. "But mostly I'm smiling because I'm amazed at God."

"God? What are you talking about? How'd we jump from my work problems to God?"

"You don't know the whole story."

"Obviously."

They turned around and began walking back toward their vehicles. Ryan told her about his visit from Matthew. "I know all that sounds kinda crazy, but he told me something that has stuck with me. He said that I was made for more than I've taken hold of."

"So … the same angel that visited Peter and Andy is now making visits to you?"

"Seems like it."

"Okay. Well, that's great, but I still don't see how that connects to my work drama."

"B, I've never stuck around to see much of anything through. When people wanted to get close to me, to really get to know me, I ran. Sometimes just from the friendship, but normally to another job or town. Then I came to Crossing and met your family. I met you. And somehow, I found the courage to stay, even when you saw through me and called me a chicken."

Brittney paused in the path and turned to look at him.

"I believe I was made for the job in Crossing," Ryan continued. "Dr. Williams and I have the same vision for the clinic." He took her hand. "All we need is a nurse with a heart for the people."

Brittney searched his face. *He wants me to move to Crossing? Work side by side with him as Nicole had suggested?*

"But there's more." He took a step closer to her. "I need something too. Not for the clinic, but for me. I need a wife who loves me and will make sure I'm not taking great care of others without taking care of myself."

She looked into his eyes. "Are you asking me something?"

He stepped as close to her as he dared, taking both her hands in his. "Brittney Yager, I've already talked to every man in your family. Pops said it was about time, Frank said he'd be honored, Logan was enthusiastic, and Peter said something about a dish throwing."

Brittney half-laughed, half-groaned.

"You'll have to explain that, but first I need you to know that I love you more than I thought it was possible for me to love anyone. Your smile invades my every thought, and I can't seem to make the simplest decision before calling to see what you think."

Brittany held her breath, barely able to contain her joy.

"What I really want to know is if you will marry me and transfer to Crossing to work beside me?"

Tears welled in her eyes as she smiled at him. "Look's like we're in for a good ol' dish throwing!"

Chapter 23

WEDDING BELLS RANG THROUGHOUT CROSSING the last Saturday in April. Two spectators watched unseen from outside the church as family and friends cheered Ryan and Brittney's appearance at the top of the steps.

The embroidery on Brittney's satin dress sparkled in the sunshine as she turned to give her new husband a kiss for all to see. Amber, Heather, and Allie all stood on descending steps in their Malibu blue, floor-length satin and organza dresses.

"Well?" said Matthew expectantly.

"Well done," said Michael. "Very well done."

"I knew he'd come through."

Michael just smiled as he watched the scene unfold before him. "How does your next assignment look?"

Matthew looked at Melody as she stood on the church stairs throwing rose petals. The unit secretary from the Doernbecher Children's Hospital pediatric oncology ward was completely unaware of what the next several months held for her. "Orders are in place. Her man finds out soon he'll be moving to 3rd Special Forces Group."

"That means moving across the country."

"Yes, North Carolina. But I believe she will go. Inside her is a childlike trust that she does not yet recognize. You will see."

Ryan, decked out in a white tux, led his bride down the church steps and through the shower of fragrant rose petals just as Peter, Logan, and Andy hurried to join the crowd of well-wishers at the base of the steps. Ryan's eyes narrowed with suspicion as he noticed the old towel the three men shared as they wiped something from their hands and grinned. Then Ryan peered beyond them and groaned.

Sunshine glistened on the white foam that now adorned his prized black Mustang.

Coming Soon!

Romancing Melody

MELODY MARRIED HER PRINCE CHARMING and journeyed with him across the country to Ft. Bragg, North Carolina. As much as she hates being 3,000 miles away from her family on the west coast, she wants to adjust to life as a soldier's wife.

Shortly after the birth of their baby, Cole, David deploys with the War on Terror and Melody settles into motherhood. She quiets her doubts and determines to make the best of Army life.

But when the unthinkable happens, where will Melody turn? Could God really be seeking her out in the midst of tragedy?

Also by Carrie Daws

CROSSING VALUES

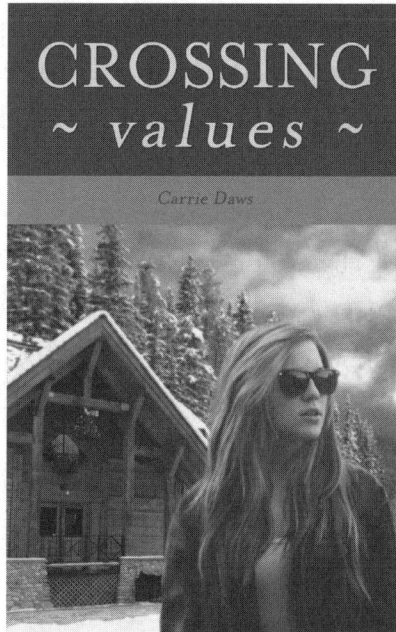

Paperback: 160 pages
ISBN: 9781935507925

FOR YEARS, AMBER TRAIPSED AROUND the Northwest avoiding the skeletons in her closet. Job-hopping every few weeks, she refused to let anyone get close to her as she slowly made her way east. As winter plants itself firmly across the Rockies, she decides to take a chance on a job at a logging company with a family different from any she's ever known before.

Watching the family interact creates more questions than answers for Amber. Feeling like she's entered the happily-ever-after written at the end of a fairytale, she watches for cracks in the facade. Surely as the days pass, the play-acting will cease and the real family will emerge.

Or could she be wrong? Could they truly be genuine? Could Faye understand the trauma from her past or Peter think of her as more than just the winter office help? Could this family really hold the key to what she's seeking?

Purchase books by Carrie Daws at:
- Amazon.com
- Barnesandnoble.com
- Christianbook.com

or other fine retail booksellers.

Ryan's Crossing Book
Club Discussion Sheet

So you want to recommend to your book club that you read Crossing Values, but then you'd be responsible for coming up with the discussion? Not a problem! Simply download the free Discussion Sheet available at CarrieDaws.com/Freebies and take it along with you.

Scan the QR code with your smartphone to download the free Crossing Values Discussion Sheet

For more information about
Carrie Daws
&
Crossing Values
please visit:

Scan the QR code with
your smartphone to visit
the author's web site

www.CarrieDaws.com
Contact@CarrieDaws.com
@CarrieDaws

For more information about
AMBASSADOR INTERNATIONAL
please visit:

www.ambassador-international.com
@AmbassadorIntl
www.facebook.com/AmbassadorIntl